Mot Bleu

Mot Bleu

A Rock and Roll Story

by

Judson Klein

The contents are based on interviews, articles published in, and events surrounding the publication of Mot Bleu, Wichita's Entertainment Journal, from 1993-1995. Because of the liberties taken in the depictions, this should be considered a work of fiction based on true stories. Many names were changed to protect a random, anonymous happening somewhere, sometime in the Midwest.

Copyright 2008 Judson Klein. All Rights Reserved.

No part of this book may be reproduced in whole or in part without the prior written express permission of the publisher.

ISBN 978-1-935382-00-3

Artwork by Wichita artist Mike Fallier
http://www.mikefallier.carbonmade.com

Contents

Chapter 1 7
Chapter 2 11
Chapter 3 15
Chapter 4 19
Chapter 5 25
Chapter 6 35
Chapter 7 37
Chapter 8 41

    Adult Civics Test I 45

Chapter 9 49
Chapter 10 53
Chapter 11 55

    Horoscope Off the Cusp 59

Chapter 12 61
Chapter 13 65
Chapter 14 71
Chapter 15 73
Chapter 16 77
Chapter 17 79

    Horoscope Off the Cusp 83

Chapter 18 85
Chapter 19 91
Chapter 20 95
Chapter 21 99

    Do you want a fun job? 100
    WELL BECOME A
    CRIMINAL!

Chapter 22 107

    Adult Civics Test II 111

Chapter 23 115
Chapter 24 121
Chapter 25 123

Chapter 1

"I tell you Jim, I'm the most conservative son of a bitch you ever met. You'll never meet a bigger one than me."

"I know, I know John, goddamn it but you still gotta be smart. You still gotta know where to put your money at. You match minds with me Joe and I'll tell you."

"Jim, I known you a long time -"

"Yeah I know but listen here John. It's all in the newsprint. A business that's been dyin' for the better half of two decades is coming back. You remember about ten years back this town was known for having one of the most strongest and progressive medias in the country until the goddamn liberals came along and dumped it all into the Arkansas River. But it's making a comeback now, and that's where all the money is going. Just look at all the new newsprint publications distributin' around town. That's where you would put your money at if you were a wise man, John. And don't let no liberal send you off on no half-assed scheme that won't do nothin' but make you look like a goddamn fool." James raised his voice so all could hear him. "Fuck all the fucking liberals who try to take everything the working man creates in this city all away."

"Jim, that sounds like a fine proposition."

"Yeah, you listen to me. It's time to say goodbye to all the sons of bitch liberals." He lifted his drink to all around him. "Goodbye Ted Kennedy, goodbye to the fucking hippies, goodbye Hillary the lesbian, In The Name Of The Father Son Holy Ghost goodbye."

"Okay Jim, that sounds fine but all I know is that I am drunk and broke now and have to go home. See you tomorrow."

Somewhere down this road there's an island in the stream / several miles that constitute a world / Like the colors in a marble / the value of a pearl...

I recall the first part of a sort of lyric that popped into my head when I entered the last of very few turns on a journey that ended long ago. But for some reason its latter phrasing escapes me. It came to me while traveling west through a vista of freshly harvested fields on a straight four-lane stretch of highway for over three hours without encountering so much as a knoll or intersection. Later at a gas station on the perimeter of the city an old man who noticed my extrinsic license plate passed onto me the first tidbit of wisdom I would need if ever I were to become the Midwestern soothsayer: *Truly you haven't come to the edge of the earth, my son, but you can see it from here.*

That same day, almost four years ago, I feared there would be a night like this. Enough is different.

On no particular evening I sit behind the barely lighted eyes of a vacant skull sipping the murky diluted brain fluid drawn from a tap jammed into its lifeless cranium by the indifferent new owners. Among the few silent patrons here I am the only one immersed in the echoes of its previous night's dream - of what this club used to be.

Here were the mortal remains of a wicked and romantic era. The new patrons were traditional enough to wear the flannel-checkered shirts and snakeskin boots (likely manufactured the same way a hundred years ago) but contemporary enough to leave the cowboy hats home. Mostly. Adept in adultery and wary of what motivated their neighbors to like a certain football team. Steadfast and proud of their pickup truck and personal niche in the industry - should they have one.

The small riser of a stage had not been moved. Only without the great horned PA speakers flanking it looked no more than a local church choir's pulpit. Upon it now the barely-respirating members of a country band churn out the latest lethargic tones of heartbreak, divorce, and self-pity through their 300-watt amplifiers before the small and vacant dance floor.

The thin dull brown-carpeted floor is now regularly vacuumed and the pallid green once covering the standard cinder block walls is a newer but less lively tan, although the myriad nicks and punctures from flyers that announced formerly upcoming bands endure like fossils underneath. The pool tables are cocked at the same angles beneath the same cheap light-beer customized tube lighting hoods. I am overjoyed to see the strands of affordable Christmas lights still pulsing out the same rhythms in the same pattern around the ceiling. The same banister with the same antiquated graffiti engravings and stools with torn seat covers circumvent the same makeshift dancing and dining area, only now no one is seated or grooving there. At the bar a handful of raw-bones stare into their drinks on what was likely this pub's busiest hour.

For a moment there are swaying and contorting silhouettes of figures with long hair, guitar necks, circles and cylinders of a drum kit, and a dash of a microphone with echoes of killers soliciting rides, twin headlights cruising alone down roads less ventured, and vertebrates in metamorphosis reverberating around me on a shadowy but highly charged ultraviolet plane.

The good ol' boys on stage drop out one by one before the opening number is done. I look about and notice the lingering strands of mentholated cigarette smoke had silently crept in to encircle me. The brain fluid is now a gloomier shade of formaldehyde in my glass. Truly this will be my last visit to this establishment.

From the same stool I watched all those stories unfold in exhilarating songs for two years I lift my elbows to the same banister one last time and close my eyes.

Chapter 2

*Cursed be he that maketh the
blind to wander out of the way. And
all the people shall say, Amen .*

Deuteronomy 27:18-20

I wonder if it was like this for Robin Hood or The Lone Ranger, he thought. But then I doubt either one of them were ever stuck like a fly on a glue strip in rush hour traffic.

In one continuing plane of steel, polyester, strange clouds and shifting triads of light as far as the human optic nerve allowed he sat in his fairly new boat-sized station wagon. A primitive form of air conditioning offered little relief from the great frying pan of pavement all around while his modern-day Moses beard lay tangled over a wide and pointed collar, and his large red globe of hair stuck to the interior roof in a damp circle. His sweaty hands slid down either side of the wide steering wheel when he saw the ambulance appear, gumballs-ablaze, from a distant street and race towards the intersection before him.

One more canvassing meeting for the afternoon, and that's a wrap for this week. Then methinks a well deserved weekend celebration is upon me. Above the twin moons of his spectacles he kept watch on the enduringly red light. He fumbled through the inside pocket of his corduroy jacket, making sure that tightly rolled sandwich bag was still there. *This new alloy may have uses they never anticipated. Now if only they made their cars just a tad smaller...*

Not far from Manhattan's post rush hour traffic was Central Park, likely the most fitting sight for a meeting of nationally organized functional dysfunctionalists. At least so thought the great many parvenus who held this city soundly in their sovereignty. The haves were getting cross with them, and that meant they were doing something right. In just the previous week he had accompanied groups of young canvassers from door to door down the shadiest lanes of Harlem in the evening hours, passing the darkest shapes in the narrowest of alleyways. Thieves surely lurked about but the small-time gangster thing was not yet en vogue. Most small-time organized crime had a sturdy revenue. Nixon was on his way out, some of the ugliest public confrontations were sliding under the public rug, and the greatest and most tragic of all police actions was finally over. *But this order of low-pressure visionaries has seen the enemy, and people of conscious and education need take up their canvassing packages.*

The strangest thing of all was how they were taken in. It was still an era of anti-culture, carnal awareness and expanding the awakened state; even at the risk of damaging one's mental well-being. And for the first time it was all given some amount of air time, and deemed a substantial threat to the establishment, depending on what state of the union you were in. It was still considered very uncouth for your average unknown white guy to knock on doors anywhere in lower-class black America, especially in Harlem, with or without invitation. Many of the powers that were were still reeling at the realization that many of their keen white offspring had - of all things - adapted some of their mannerisms while changing portions of culture. Like the music.

But they were never turned away. In all four of his years serving as canvass director he never received so much as a dirty look, even on the latest of evenings in the most foreboding blocks of seemingly lifeless housing. Even when they would intervene on a group of boozed-up Negroes (the phrase African-American was in its earliest stages of recognition) raging around a black and white television they were always heard out. How to recognize the corporate fist coming down and who to talk to when it lands. How to know what health care options were open to them. How to make unwarranted evictions and substandard living conditions a thing of the past. What was wrong in the community and how to find other people that share the same concerns. Where to get valuable information on legal assistance and health care options. Simple, painless, non-time consuming ways to organize for a better standard of living. The presentation was always kept as brief as possible and thank-yous always exchanged.

But on this afternoon social reform or teaching the poor how to tidy up whatever community did not have priority. When he reached the park he would collect the day's work and get primed for some heavy meditation.

There has to be a benign ruler in all of this somewhere, but if he or she doesn't turn up soon then someone has to flush them out of hiding. If only I could make a little more cash working for the little guy. For now I'll have to get stoned and think about our next move...

Then he saw the ambulance, its sirens wailing, weaving through the deadlocked traffic at about 50 mph. When the lissome hearse-like white vehicle reached the intersection in front of him he watched it pause to make a left-hand turn.

Then it happened. A long and Cimmerian black Sedan simply darted out behind it and took over the center lane. It accelerated in a straight and narrow course as cars in its path veered off and into numerous fender benders. Just when the ambulance paused to turn, the Sedan gained a length on it and filled the intersection before him. As the dark automobile arched far left he saw the long dark locks of the Hasidic Jews slant with it, leaving the ambulance to slam on its brakes and veer hard into the compact Japanese vehicle next to it, stalling out.

Was that an omen? Far was it from Tom Willy to be candidly religious or superstitious. But he continued to look down the adjoining street long after the light above turned green, and the horns sounded behind him.

Chapter 3

"Somewhere I had come up with the notion that one's personal life had nothing to do with fiction, when the truth, as everyone knows, is nearly the direct opposite."
— Thomas Pynchon

IF you are a native or historian of the great Midwest, you might still imagine the horseback trailblazers who once pounded the pathways your car now glides over, braving life and limb to establish one of the earliest forms of civility nationwide - a taxable mail route. But as mass communication evolved the romance was lost and postcards morphed into e-mail and billboards; speedier forms of communication instantly firing messages of great and menial significance.

In cities of greater topography you might miss many of them behind overpasses or troughs in the road. But here you could see them coming at you one after another for miles - the voluptuous kittens with sunken cheeks fondling slim cigarettes and giving you just as much time to read them as your range of sight allowed. Gasoline. Eat. Smoke this. Giant cowboys grinning over semi-functional neon hotel signs. Every incarnation of denim ever. Another Eat. Carnal dancing that just may push its legal parameters, provided you've got the right bill or candy. I later learned that a great many coming-of-age area girls here actually aspired for that kind of work, feeling little shame in making money off a long-standing tradition. Once Wichita was a stop-off for the great cowboys who drove their herds of cattle out of Texas as far north as Minnesota. When the doggies retired it was time for drinking and debasing women for as long as their wages allowed, creating some of the most cherished but somewhat insipid folklore Gloria Steinem would not touch with a 100-foot phallic symbol. They may as well have run helium-filled love dolls mouths-agape up flagpoles. But it will always be there for your consumption, so eat it all up, man. Eat it. Eat.

Symbols of the American motif were everywhere - grinning Jayhawks or other sports logos on clothing and cars, massive trucks bearing down on the highway, obese city workers relaxing around a dilapidated exit ramp, and alcohol monarchs making their obsequious associations around every corner, visible in one incarnation or another at all times.

But goddammit (notice the lower case, my redeemer) it was still America. Later I was to receive a group scowl in one of the city's more posh country bars for ordering an imported beer.

But then I threaded a fly over and it was all gone. It was like some ancient parchment was suddenly unrolled before me, the earth upturned in all directions, every third mile or so marked off by a single row of slender trees like huge dried mushrooms sometimes clustered around tiny farmhouses in the distance. Truly this was the basket that bore the bread. It seemed not a square inch was left unwanting for the coming season – overturned and ready for planting. One side of the fly over was dependent on the other, in both economics and way of life. And perhaps through all the strategic marketing and slightly abject perversity of the latter terrain the land did maintain a sense of gracefulness and generosity, with the far-away farmer atop his red 1970s tractor amidst miles of the nation's largest sky. The earthy aroma of freshly reaped soil was the finishing touch on what could be the most quaint, complacent and totally flat aesthetic in the known universe.

I looked over my shoulder just in time to see the shiny silver Eagle Talon gaining on me. A burly Mennonite whose trousered belly and grey beard filled the driver's side of his car blew by me in the passing lane, turning a bespectacled visage towards me and lifting a wooly-white hand to make some sort of one-fingered gesture I could not make out but did guess its definition. From that moment on, on every stretch of Kansas road I traveled, some large pickup loomed in my rearview mirror, teetering to pass. The vehicle vanished into the sunset ahead.

Chapter 4

I firmly believe that any man's finest hour, the greatest fulfillment of all that he holds dear, is that moment when he has worked his heart out in a good cause and lies exhausted on the field of battle - victorious.
             -Vince Lombardi Legendary Greenbay Packers coach

HERE they come. On the fields off of what little hillside there was they came in eights or twelves of a color. Guided by one figurehead on the field and galvanized by the Omni-present spectators in the stands. Just one or two wisps of exhale in the cold were the greatest mentors in the masses. *Come on, son. Succeed. Live my dream.* For they were the newly reborn egos, just old enough to be justifiably pissed off and symbolically homicidal; this year's valiant warriors of the great and enduring metaphor, for all the ephemeral honor in the world is at stake tonight.

You could hear the collective vehemence from the opposing stands when that first buzzer sounded. The unseen commentator greeted the crowd over a small PA horn speaker mounted outside his tower while the small-time reporter stood on the sideline of the home team with his play sheets, notebook and camera, trying not to be distracted by the chain of cheerleaders in their brightly monotone uniforms and often creeping panties they flashed in those traditional kicks – innocent visual titillation. This I sometimes found more interesting than the game itself.

In the poorly lit hallways of imitation marble and rows of cost-worthy lockers they were the man-boys and woman-girls of great virtue and caliber. Their trophies of achievement remained behind glass for as long as their miniature fortress stood, reminders of the glorious romps recently and long ago, even though the Spartans of yesterday had faded with the newsprint or were now in the stands cheering on a new crop of champions they sired themselves.

Eventually Johnny's days of valor would fade into the less chivalric setting of frat parties and beer guzzling contests. He hung out in kids-coming-of-age clubs where the wealthy but drunken aftermath of the yuppie generation clung to the bar and blew their allowances while the gleaming, puerile, threshold-of- parenthood girls swapped the most sinful of tales. *You got some catching up to do, missy* was heard on occasion.

But that was all just the future - unconcerning and hardly substantial. Right then and there he was outstanding amidst his peers and elders; adept in abstinence (as far as they knew) and earning esteem. Nothing could stop a young man from breaking the planes he aimed for. Of Christian decent substantial enough not to cheat on his girlfriend of an equally fine breeding - at least not with anyone finding out. Johnny regularly gave thanks to the Lord Jesus Christ for a winning game or season while his opponents wrapped their elbows and scratched their bruised noggins wondering where they went wrong in prayer. The stands were filled with his fans elbow to elbow, the less motivated classmates and adults-by-day yearning for the collective validation of their cause. And I made sure he became the hero they wanted.

It was the year of our Lord 1993 and there I was, this wayward journalist, fresh out of college with a rudimentary outline of his chosen profession. Another small-time reporter toggling the valve of another small information outlet for another small chronic waterfall of ongoing metaphorical statistics for new-but-the-same suburban weekend warriors who hung on every number, as if a victory for their home team was a moral victory for themselves, or proved them a virtuoso among their friends in some tribal art of the ego. I was their very objective watchdog always at the end of his chain with his nose up to the breeze. Legend upon legend was born doing the same thing as the folklore stood the test of time. And damn I looked good behind that marred mahogany desk with my geek-ass haircut and skinny blue tie, rolling newsprint into symbolic joints and wondering if I had any chance at all with the newest crop of 18-year old pep squad gals. Our mysterious moustached publisher sat grinning in his office as we pegged away on our cheap low-resolution word processors, not missing a stem of that year's economic and political yield as it came and withered. Our bespectacled California-native surfer archetype editor monitored us close, often scowling and sometimes shaking his head as if with sympathy, knowing his evangelical practices, neo-conservative angle and glorification of business tycoons who have crushed their competition and exploited their employees would someday take him and his darling wife and child to the luxury suite beyond the toils of suffering lesser-minded infidels like myself. It was a transient test of endurance. There would be eternal front and center seats to monitor the glory of all warriors who crush the competition. Then a post-game pizza party with the apostles and a mountain of meat, hosted by God and His Son in football jerseys. He did not seem to realize his home state was the birthplace of some of the finest anti-culture in U.S. history, including psychedelic drug experimentation, open homosexuality, and other things that would certainly not earn Jesus' stamp of approval. Never did he mention the Grateful Dead or Ken Kesey.

The more things changed the more we wrote the same so-called stories. The military was cranking out war machines locally to protect us. It would help the economy grow. The local football team going to state semi-finals was cause for prayer and pilgrimage. The church bake sale pulling in top dollar was divine intervention. Someone franchising a new carpet store was huge news. I had a feeling the following year would be no different.

Until *phone for you on line four* our plump-in-plaid receptionist called over the intercom.

Chapeau Recorder sports desk this is your local sports reporter.

"Hello. This is Tom, curator of the great liberal presses in America, returning your call."

When your senses connect with your unspoken personal purposes it becomes physical. I lunged forward in my chair and went totally pro. This was my chance to do something besides board of education, capitalism and sports stories. Not that I minded giving the kids a keepsake for a lifetime. I certainly enjoyed hanging with and writing about them, but the fans were another matter entirely. I wondered if they would ever know what truly motivated their own offspring – how important it was to them to please their parents.

Yes, I've been a big fan of your magazine since it came out *fibs for the sake of a profession are okay* and it looks like your content is right up my alley of writing. I was wondering if you needed to expand your reporting staff at all. I am a fully educated and professional journalist with strong editorial and layout skills-

"Are you a democrat or a republican."

--Irish Catholic G.O.P. All the way, sir, full registered. *Which meant I had no idea what a Republican was when I registered, though the conservative approach is always the safest* But I have strong creative and editorial skills and can bring new angles to your publication that I think, um, people will really be interested in. I'm sure my ideas would thus expand your readership and subsequently your advertising market. If you would like I will send a full resume and clippings-

"Have you ever read *The Hawkline Monster* by Richard Brautigan?"

Nearly forgotten images of a living elephant's foot umbrella stand and sensual, enigmatical, and often naked twin Indian girls lit up before my eyes.

...Yes, as a matter of fact I have, a long time ago. Man, that was one wild read.

"Good. Do you know who Hunter S. Thompson and Ken Kesey are?"

More images-ambiguous. This time of a more abstract and unsorted era in my life.

"Why yeah, in college I read *Fear and Loathing in Las Vegas* about twice and *The Electric Cool-Aid Acid Test* about...about..."

"Fine. Then why don't you write me up something and send it to the address listed in the magazine's masthead beneath the credits. I won't be able to pay you a lot at first, but I'm sure we can work something out eventually."

And so it was. I forfeited my lunch break to hammer out some quick observances I made during my college radio - disc jockey years on the growth of pop music in the latter decade and decline of the "underground" scene, using the same terminal that got Johnny all those girls. This was my big chance to do some *really* objective reporting. Maybe give platform to those less spoken of but more deserving for their interpretation and metaphor, in a forum far less concerned with virtue and victory.

The California archetype walked by, his expression unchanged. He must have thought I was deep into some perfunctory sports coverage. Little did we both know.

Chapter 5

RODNEY *waited to receive honors. As people filed into the stadium he stood sternly in full uniform, his vision fixed straight ahead with imitation rifle shouldered and helmet shined to the mirror-like standard. It was not just a day of graduation but one of transformation, accomplishment, degree and right of passage to the uncompromising and never-ending challenges that lie ahead. The days of dorm parties and prissy make-up laden girls were over. Today he received the scepter of manhood. It had also been a sure-fire way of affording school. When his division leader seemed occupied he broke his gaze and looked towards the gates. Inside people filed in, in family units, contributing to the growing but ever subtle murmur, while somewhat of a rancor seemed to be swelling but not crossing the threshold outside.*

Sometimes the center does hold. Out of the three blocks of elegantly stenciled display windows and fine archaic craftsmanship above smooth sidewalks, the quaintly designed lampposts turned into knotted industrial streetlights towering overhead, parallel to increasingly nondescript housings. If you were an eastbound traveler who could not afford the spoils of downtown clubs and restaurants you drove towards one of the few inclinations in the city, where the rent and food was more affordable. Up the small ramp-like road winding through smudges of shrubbery growing in squares of stained amber chips stood a green dash of street sign to commemorate the phenomenon - Hillside Avenue.

Remnants of Wichita's first governing district dominated the hill. The formerly prestigious abodes of long ago were now housings for college kids and newcomers. Down the street marquees fluttered above coffee shops, quaint clothing stores and small one-room restaurants.

One of these housings was just around the first curve on the hill. The three-floored faded amber brick structure nestled fast into the slanting ground like the regal grandmother of a century past, glaring through multi-framed glasses at the tiny corporate taco shop sprung up just a few doors down. This huge relic was the headquarters for the city's Scientology assembly, whose clientele appeared to be exclusively privileged.

Across the street a carpeted porch angled around the bottom floors of a small quad of apartments. The entire structure – its modest siding, shingles, and trim, was painted white, as if its usual inhabitants of college kids tried to project decency or innocence as the rest of the city watched them closely.

In the small gravel parking lot behind it signs threatened to tow your unauthorized ass. *Like I'm terrified. The neighbors probably won't mind when their dealer comes over looking for a place to park. Now, which door is it?* On the bottom floor, almost right on the lot, sky blue curtains parted behind a thin pane on a chipped white door with a speckled brass knob. On the window was another sign. The Keeper of The Plains, the city icon, a Seneca tribe chief caricature with full headdress, arched his back and raised his palms in prayer or pain above the skyline of tall downtown buildings. Only this one clutched a microphone. Underneath him arced two words: *Mot Bleu.* The entire door rattled as I knocked on the wood.

With a squeak the door opened inward. Pools of violet bloomed while my eyes adjusted, before darkness and color created Tom Willy. The spectacles came first, then the leaden beard, brow and receded grey curls above the pinstriped and open collar. Then came the narrow leather buckle belt and chestnut dress slacks. But the opening in the doorway only suited one.

Hi, I'm the sports reporter who sent you that résumé package the other week, extending a hand in the most professional manner I could muster.

"Hi. I'm Tom." We shook hands over the threshold. "So, you live in Wichita all your life?"

Well no, actually I rode here from the east coast about two years ago and have been working as a sports writer since -

The portal then opened wide and Tom Willy stood aside, arm extended to his apartment.

"In that case come right in! You don't mind my wariness of radiation. Or anyone who's lived within a few hundred miles of this town for too long. God knows what chemicals or isotopes they've been exposed to."

No sir, I said as I walked in. Suddenly it felt as if I had entered a sort of shelter from an unspoken paranoia or ambiguity. Something innate, indigenous; something I didn't realize until stepping into the room. Here seemed to be a shelter from a tradition that needed serious objective review. I felt like great stories would be written within these walls that a yet latent culture was yearning to hear.

"Hey, you know what they say about an ounce of precaution and pound of repair. Would you like a drink?" he said, the grin unaffected. I drove by a chemical plant each day on my way to the Chapeau office, a distant setting from Dante's poem with slim iron minarets ceaselessly bellowing bluish smoke and vapor into the big sky. So I could hardly blame someone for worrying about pollution.

Sure!

I handed him the copy - typeset and written in standard Associated Press style, spell checked with perfect margins double-spaced and slick as a motherfucker. I saw the angled characters in a plane of white reflect off his lenses. I supposed he was reading, though I could not see his eyes skim the words beneath the glare. His expression stayed unchanged. Then he peered over the wiry rims at me.

"Alright. This sounds pretty rad." His pupils sank back down into the black and white. "Good. We used to have this saying, it was pretty funny at the time - The movement has been subverted by a deviant culture; and they are our masters now."

I frowned, puzzled. He reached to the edge of a small collapsible kitchen table with one leaf down for a glass containing what looked like iced-down ether. He then brought up a soft velvet foldout file case with a brass latch in front. He opened it and pulled out a cigarette.

Then it happened, right before my eyes. There was kind of a soundless rumble as the glass came down below a contracted, grey expression. It was pure transformation. In assiduous lethargy his head turned my way - a setup for a visage I would not soon forget - a glowing grin behind aged whiskers, chin bowed nearly to his sternum as narrow slits slanted an unspoken sagastic acumen right through me. Then the ecstatic pause.

"I hope you don't think you're the first generation of youngsters that try to be different or express their discontent about anything."

Man, I bet you saw the whole anti-culture thing begin blossom and probably fade out, from beginning to end.

"Oh," he said, "I think you could put it like that."

The campus spread wide for him that day. The roadways and intermittent greenery rolled slightly between sovereign buildings with myriad paned windows rebounding the afternoon sun, constructed in a semi-circle through a network of brick pathways and catwalks. Suits and briefcases ambled freely alongside sweaters, bell-bottoms and skirts, creating a scene nothing short of academic, hygienic and tranquil.

There he stood before the entrance gates of the collegiate sports arena, the sun shooting rainbow prisms off his spectacles and his huge Afro like frayed Irish fire over a bushy brow and beard of an equal brilliance. Echoes of the gunfire that claimed four student's lives four years previous and tones of a Jefferson Airplane song leading a chant of "REVOLUTION!" resonated in the air all around them, even for those who dodged through the disdain to respectfully attend the ceremony. And they were not about to let up.

The college had tried moving the event. They even tried advertising a false day for the ceremony. But by the time the ROTC graduation was in full pomp and circumstance the parking lot was nearly full of collectively disordered college kids. Banners of accusation and inquietude were lifted to the highest reaches of the human form and passed along to all, smoke rising from cigarettes and joints, resembling a plateau of hair and flowers from the top seats of the stadium.

When the ceremonies concluded the barrage began. They tried sneaking the new cadets out through the locker room exits but Kent State didn't recruit dummies. They were met with an onslaught of verbal ridicule, cans, stones and whatever else would fly. The undergrad ROTC cadets tried to divide the crowd but were mostly absorbed into its mass.

Tom Willy took the last bite of his apple. He turned it over in his hand and eyed the seed protruding from the ruptured core. He then heaved it in an arc over the heads of his comrades and heard the distinct ping of it connecting with a silvery helmet, leaving one unsightly slippery splat.

"*There, baby killer,*" *he howled, fist raised high. "Howaboutthat food for thought!*"

The ice cubes jangled as the glass came down.

But don't you think the kids who went into service at the time should be honored and respected for making the supreme sacrifice, so people like yourself did not have to go?

"Yeah," he responded unfaltering, "but it was a popular thing to do at the time. You know, with kids chaining themselves to the capital's gates and stuff."

I considered. He flew into further tales of a higher education system that was nearly shut down, psychedelic drugs, orgies in dorm rooms with Quaaludes handed out at the door, and police chasing himself and a friend through a crowded bar of kids who immediately clustered together, separating hunter from quarry.

He suddenly lobbied, knotting his brow and administering the look. "Who's Bhutros Bhutros Ghali."

Oh I know I damn mean I knew some really important Euro dictator overseas -

"Former Secretary General of the United Nations. Possibly the worst one we've ever had." The look remained fixed upon me.

Right on. Hey my parents told me that was the most frightening era they could remember. Especially for anyone trying to raise a young family.

"Yeah, something like that. It was a pretty heavy time. But it's not like Kent was the first. There were numerous Ivy League schools that actually had students armed with rifles, like Harvard or Brown I think, but nothing became of it. The police waited them out, and were like, 'okay we'll put in black studies or cut back on ROTC funding,' but none of them wanted to take shots at senators' sons and daughters. You don't hear a lot about that. It was a bunch of weekend warriors that popped the caps at

Kent. They had just burned down the ROTC building and were cutting up the fire hoses with axes as they tried to put out the blaze. Governor Rhodes had been saying things like, 'Okay, no more gatherings' to calm them down, but then he called in the National Guard the next day. They were just a bunch of part-time grunts who didn't know it was just a few hundred of them against a several thousand college kids until they decided to charge right through. That's when they suddenly came to a fence. They had to turn around and wade back through the crowd...I don't know what happened, someone yelled something or some guardsman took a warning shot that the rest of them thought came from some kid, but it resulted in that famed 27 seconds. But that was far, far from the first stand off. It just had a less pleasant finale."

The ice cubes jangled as the glass came down. The grin had descended as well. He had turned so the light sparkled off only one arm of his spectacles. He then returned the twin resolute fissures to me; my mouth slightly agape in the generic expression of: Whoa.

"What is 'The Night of Sorrow?'"

Later on when we're out of money for booze??

"No. It's the night in 1968 when students on a Mexican campus protesting for human rights were shot down by their government, no questions asked. It was kept under wraps for years...What is N.A.F.T.A?'"

I raised my brow.

"Don't worry, you're not the only one. But I regress. You want to talk about submitting something every month? I can't pay you much until I build up the advertising dollar, but I can give you a list of clubs in town if you want to make rounds, and cover the local band scene." He set the glass back down on the edge of the table, the perfectly round plane of booze pendulating above the slowly turning ice cubes. He opened the case and riffled several papers before suddenly looking up, his spectacles catching the glare again. "...You've probably seen those pictures of kids putting flowers in the rifle barrels."

Yes. I've seen black and white stills of them.

"That was the subtlest gesture - telling a row of soldiers, 'Here! Don't shoot us! Have some flowers.' But it's nothing like that today. The only option we have now is to get as wacky and demented as we can possibly get. I think in that regard we're going to do some serious damage in this town."

It's okay, thought Rodney, his hard-shell still ringing from the impact. They just don't want to face up to the true responsibilities of life. Besides, that's nothing compared to a round of mortar in the noggin.

Leave it to Beavis

"And up next, we're going to see some videos that don't suck. There, I said it. SUCK! Okay, SUCK!"

A true milestone in television history. After decades of correspondents going behind the German Lines of WWII, into the jungles of Vietnam, and bringing live footage of the moon and supernovas into our living rooms, the MTV veejays have kicked down the doors of sexual repression and liberated the work suck.

The Federal Communications Commission has given way to more stimulating advertising hooks that will surely sell, as the censors appear to be brushing their dentures in media nursing homes.

Long ago the Pony Express was replaced by the telegraph, which was replaced by radio, which was improved to television, which is now entering uncharted digital territory.

In all this time trends and personalities became recognized across much of the world, and the great gatekeepers of the media had to decide what they should let into living rooms of American Families. What would be information, what would be entertainment, and what would rot their minds or persuade them to step out of line? What would piss of God?

So the FCC claimed to own the magnetic air around us. Someone had to keep this powerful tool out of the hands of madmen. Airtime was divided up, and only those concerned with the better interests of society could broadcast. Hence the term *social responsibility* was spawned.

Every possible degree of thought somehow manifested itself on film. German film makers would create the most abstract reel-to-reel art films, pornographic takes were knows as "smokers," and eventually even some of the bloodiest wartime moments were captured.

But none of it could be seen on television. Since then the FCC has loosened its grip on what goes onto the screen. At one point censorship became a dirty word, and people began looking for a national speaker's pulpit to be heard. Ask the American Civil Liberties Union, they will tell you all about it.

Some say the great hippie and peace movements of the 1950s and 1960s came after people actually saw what was going on behind the lines, when images of Korea and Vietnam were brought into their homes. Only a handful of reporters brought us images that still stand as landmarks in history.

Did the hippies finally make war unpopular? Even though decades of small town cinema war propaganda may have come to an end, it is hard to imagine it was ever genuinely popular.

Thousands of reporters flocked east for the Gulf War, only to find certain areas of battle closed to them. Were they just in the way, or was it something more?

It is obvious the images on the screen can move us on a grand scale, but it is now becoming apparent they may touch us even deeper - especially at younger, more impressionable ages.

Some people admit to having roll models. Others resign only to their own identities, and these are often the deepest waters of all, while others simply pick and choose identities for a secure foundation in life.

Regardless, there is an endless menu of personalities made ready for us on television. And kids, in search of a recognized, effective persona, can easily pick up on them. Psychologists say there is undisputable evidence of media swaying behavior, and it is tough to argue with them.

Fictional characters cannot only be easy to identify with but to emulate. What is a sport? Investing hopes and fears in a team looking to score.

Look at the money wrapped up in it. Catch phrases such as "Just Do It" and "Why Ask Why" have woven themselves into our vocabularies, phrases that essentially tell one not to think of anything and just buy this product.

Some children go to the film "The Program" and are later run over while lying in the middle of the road. Beavis persuades children to burn down their houses. Isolated instances? Perhaps. But have you ever met anyone who thinks they belong in a soap opera drama? A fanatic who cannot see sports as just a metaphor for the painstaking process of becoming something greater? Kids pretending to be Darth Vader?

Perhaps the true meaning of social responsibility has become somewhat obscured. Perhaps people were never told how to make good of repressed animosity, pay attention to what was really happening in the world, and media from television to billboards telling them they have to have something every day did not help.

Regardless, it appears (one would hope) that people are becoming fed up with Buttafucos, overpaid actors compromising their art for sleazy scenes, murderous cartoon characters, fleshy blue jean commercials and mass produced compulsion for the sake of someone making a buck. Broadcasters don't have to simulate violence anymore; they just have to follow the police around for a night.

The Beavers and Andy Griffiths of television are gone, old archetypes that will never likely return as they were. Still, if we no longer have taboos on what we see on the screen, if it is or is not representing something that is really happening, perhaps we should at least evaluate the motives for cramming it down our throats each day.

Chapter 6

"The hitch-hiker stood up and looked across through the windows.
'Could ya give me a lift, mister?'
The driver looked quickly back at the restaurant for a second.
'Didn't you see the No Riders sticker on the win'shield?'
'Sure - I seen it. But sometimes a guy'll be a good guy even if
some rich bastard makes him carry a sticker.'"

- The Grapes of Wrath
John Steinbeck

THERE I was. The road roaring under my engine and oncoming vee-hickles whisking by, the sole colossal vista spread wide and only growing larger before me - hopped aboard a jet stream and headed into it's heart like a literary bullet of verse and velocity. Little trial and tribulation loomed in my dust, like most recent grads, but still I felt the pages of another impeding and lethargic (even though I had been making decent money) chapter turn over behind me. Turn over on the incessant struggle to achieve within the parameters of industrial values and be recognized by my alleged superiors. Deadlines, frustration, and the California Archetype – who bumped me out of the sports department so he could monitor his favorite and not-so-favorite paladins. To again raise platform for Yin by means of Yang. His chivalric bow to the anima of Mother Nature, aesthetic in all her beauty as a scorpion's tail slips from underneath leafy her gown to snuff out species by the thousands. He was again the master of keeping moguls grinning and their subjects divided and pissed off at each other in the name of our good Lord. A great rationalization but still I got canned.

At least I no longer had to listen to his haranguing. A typical day was hearing him blast the Beach Boys on his huge boom box while pounding out tales of Christian virtue and the monetary rewards God has granted the right. Often he clenched his Hawaiian shirt and gritted his teeth whenever I borrowed the sacred pronoun "dude." I wondered if God would mind being called dude, perhaps I would ask him some day. I could hear it in the back of his skull whenever he leaned his Monkeys - cut bespectacled surfer-boy visage in to speak with me - *This one's going to Hell. Jesus has spoken; toast this blasphemer like a marshmallow, with all his liberal buddies. He probably even protests war.*

So the gutted fields and towering white grain elevators sliding along the great open sky were either opening wide to reveal something better or were closing in to smother me for good. But in my eternal optimism I figured that no one ever got rich working for someone else, and hopefully I had learned all the necessary lessons up to that moment. It felt great. For a minute, as the silhouetted minarets released their begrimed loads into the amber city skyline, I believed in the American Dream.

Chapter 7

SLANTING. Every one of them, at some point in the day. The shadows of old buildings beneath the huge sky were all of some rectangle or cubic shape, but late in each afternoon they would bleed upon each other in various darkening abstract mélanges, and gradually stretch to their greatest lengths before disappearing into the night.

Seldom was anyone seen walking or riding a bicycle anywhere near the street, day or night. If you needed sign of real Homo Sapiens life you had to squint past the glare on the windshields of passing cars or find places to listen to the shrieks and laughter of the children, their watercolor images flickering behind the tall linked playground fences surrounding a small and pallid brick school, while the population of registered sex offenders silently grew around them.

But if you knew the city, you knew that in all its vast emptiness it was still the wellspring of some of the first gloriously tainted mythology in the nation - Americana pop culture in its genuine form. Once, in the mid-20th Century, they could not keep young people off the street. Finally after generations of playing ball, studying, and growing up just like mom and dad it was hip to be a teenager. And it felt great. Back when the grass was a little greener and the paint a little more fresh, each evening was announced by the sound of engines revving and running east and west on Douglas Street, the median strip in town. Girls in curiously short and brightly colored dresses stood with straws between small lips outside one of the abundant malt shops, long before the term morbid obesity was coined, eyeing the road for the long fins of newly purchased or restored cars (preferably a Chevy), driven by the right boy with the right kind of greased back hair, the right look, and the appropriate cool manner. As the shadows grew long and light thickened everywhere, everyone (save the usual wallflowers) were granted that moment of possible hook-up before curfews elapsed. It was called dragging the strip, in an era of valiant football heroes, leather, bobby pins, semi-hollow body guitars and astonishingly suggestive radio songs. The first signs of backlash on you, mom and dad. It was an innocence that need not be critiqued by the more contemptible elders of the preceding generation, for it was happening by itself, plucked from the tree of knowledge by its own participants, a trend that prevailed until decades later, when the police upgraded their pursuit vehicles and put a halt to the racing that left long ugly tread marks on the newly laid tar and asphalt. Still the good ol' boys endured, sitting at home with their American-brewed beer and Patsy Cline records guffawing at the antics of their less responsible children, just like their offspring do today, at the same kitchen tables.

Little was sung about those who lingered after high school or drifted into town trying to avoid the draft. Or the bloodshed and brawls that happened in the central streets after hours - working hours, that is. I once encountered an above-middle-aged fellow who passed unto me a long tale about one of these altercations. He said that inside some of the great industrial wheels of the time employees worked out a kind of caste system for different degrees of skill; assigning colors for beginner, intermediate, and Samurai master classes of labor. The lifetime employees, who were spared the more laborious tasks of the workplace, enjoyed the privilege of talking down to their subordinates. And seeing how they were usually older, bigger and a lot more feeble-witted, these jibes usually led to non-spectator showdowns after hours on the street. Pregnant gum-gnawing girlfriends or wives were often present to mediate. So the lower newcomers usually got pulverized and assumed to be the lesser males wallowing at the rear of the pack.

That is, he claimed, until the subordinate colors discovered guerrilla warfare. He said he and his fellow subordinates began jumping their alleged superiors as they stepped from their late 1950s model Chevies, body slamming them backwards over the steel window frames of open doors, creating serious work for local chiropractors and EMTs. Near the turn of the decade, when the aggressors discovered they were losing their edge, all facets of this tradition disappeared. Were this full of verisimilitude or not, I would never know, but it was a good story. And judging from the endless tales of domestic and barroom violence it was not hard to believe.

Around the same time the crowds, cruising and hang-outs diminished, the kids that didn't make it out of town lagged behind, families of their own tucked beneath the sheets inside their fading-paint households while they went out weekend nights to be with people like themselves, swapping the same fables and aspirations. There were plenty of such places around town. You just had to know where to go, for few of them could afford billboard signs looming over the road or quarter page ads in the phone book. During the day it was hard to tell if such dwellings offered business of any kind, or were just more quadrangular stone buildings harboring the ghosts of a finer forgotten time. But if you had any inkling of social archeology, or were just in the right place at the right time, you would find a culture that very much lived in the shadows, thriving in its isolation from the norm.

And a lot of the time, there will be bands.

Chapter 8

"Now then, thought I, unconsciously rolling up the sleeves of my frock, here goes for a cool, collected dive at death and destruction, and the devil fetch the hindmost."
- Moby Dick
Herman Melville

AS the color and clouds drew in, the stars unfolded like the retracting dome of some phenomenal, almost admission-free observatory, unveiling one of the most spectacular views of the heavens one could get from Planet Earth. You could look up and around until your neck grew sore and still you could not take it all in at once. It was then you knew why they called this the air capital of America.

But down here all you got was the occasional streetlight and glowing slivers underneath drawn blinds along Maple Street, just one block south of Douglas Street, where the fabled drag racing took place decades ago. Anonymously, among the non-descript dwellings was a building like a large cinder block, where through a lone display window four vacuum cleaners posed silently behind faded stenciled lettering. Above twin metal doors next to it four hooded arm lights angled over a yellow bulletin sign, suggesting some kind of activity in this perfectly cubic, perfectly featureless structure. The characters announced some band, with a name referring to some species of weasel, was playing tonight.

Around 8 p.m. you could see the cars pulling into the unlit parking area west of the structure. At nightfall the cars began pulling in one at a time, sometimes only one headlight bobbing over the rutted asphalt at a time, sometimes severed exhaust pipes blaring. Faces unfolded from the darkness as they passed the display window of the near-antique vacuum cleaner shop and came into the limited range of the four rusted lights; guys and gals in pairs or groups of three, and singular figures walking faces down with a gig bag slung over the shoulder or drum casings in hand. Still outside you could not make out much of what they looked like. Just silhouetted person shapes flickering briefly on the display window of the vacuum shop as they angled around the sharp brick corner to the main entrance, a single dented steel door, where you could make out three words painted above it long ago without much articulation - *The Rusted Bullet.*

The door held a flaking brass knob. Through there you could get a better look at them but not much. The Christmas tree lights near the ceiling pursued each other in a near perfect square, the sickly turquoise cinder blocks allowing just enough room for customers, a bar, and two bathroom doors. The guys' door hung crooked on one hinge while the girls' room was sealed away in secrecy.

Two pool tables sat in front of a bar a little longer than three open-arms. A perpendicular banister separated them from the small stage area, where massive and dark horned PA speakers flanked a humble foot and one-half tall riser. A coil of wire ran along the floor from the stage to the mixing board, inside the small area with tables. Here a balding stout and ever voiceless soundman slid levers under the tiny arched lampposts over his many-channeled mixing board.

If there was just a little more lighting I would have noticed it immediately - the hundreds of flyers, mostly on legal sized paper - cut, pasted, and photocopied covered wall to wall announcing bands that were here and will come again. The larger few that made no claim to a city must have spawned in Wichita.

Not a square inch on the walls was without graffiti - runny black spray paint, crude etchings of Weasel lyric, symbol and things I didn't recognize. Yet.

By 9:30 p.m. the little room had almost reached it's capacity for comfort. The very ordinary folk in ordinary flannel shirts and faded jeans milled from table to table, laughing and chattering, the most amiable social intercourse I had witnessed in Kansas to that day. And just about all of them, regardless of their mostly lesser ages, had beer. It later occurred to me there were no well-known outlets to local music that did not associate with alcohol, and it is likely no different today.

I hesitated to leer at the girls. I was out of my usual vanity's happy hour element. Would their folks mind if I didn't make a lot of money? Did the usual cliché pick-up lines work? I put my hand to my mouth, watching and realizing. They were the repercussion and the surplus, the post-rebellion without a cause and innocence lost. Born into no great wars, depressions or winning circles of class warfare to let them know just who they were.

All previous forms of expression seemed now passé, from the extreme to the in-between, leaving them kind of stragglers without a fad ambling in circles around the central table area of this tiny Kansas pub. They seemed all in somewhat good spirits; their stringy, unstyled hair and jeans not too tight like an unspoken uniform. Perhaps it was a new natural look. Or maybe not, with the not-so-carefully layered makeup failing to completely cover the premature age lines and dark circles beneath the young ladies' eyes, minor flaws in the hue of dangling cigarettes.

From this crowd emerged Mouse. A youth out of school by the tenth grade and on to higher learning on the streets, completely unstimulated by classes and totally baffled as to how someone could get off on a poet named Homer. Like, duh. He seemed to materialize before the small crowd and approached my spot at the banister, hand extended, eager to greet this newcomer. A lone metal stud perched upon his bottom lip complimented his dirty blonde hair and joker grin. Through most of the time I knew Mouse the index finger of his right hand was always at the tiny metal marble, pointing to it whenever he spoke, drank, or sat complacent, grinning at all times. I could not make out the eye color through the reddened, narrow slits of lids.

"Hey, dude, wassup???" He was immediately cheerful. "Dude, like, these guys are so fucking cool, like, I'm sure you will like them, so like, sit back and chill and you will groove, you know?" I shared a few loud laughs and beverages with my new friend. Mouse, likely no more than 19, had no trouble ordering drinks.

I didn't think places like this were still around.

"Yeah, dude, like they're carding at all the other bars now. Like, I used to hang out all over town and drink, now here is the only place I can go to get a brew."

I hear they're cracking down.

"No doubt, man, like I've seen cops in here a couple times already." He briefly frowned, his finger still attached to the ring. "They're gonna start bustin' kids before long. It's like, if I can get drafted and go to war why can't I have a beer, you know?"

Won't be long before Big Brother brings the hammer down again, right?

"No shit?" he said, befuddled. "Like, there's a cop in your family?"

Around us several of them flipped through pages of college texts and scribbled into notebooks. I wondered how many of them would actually finish school. They likely struggled to find balance between jobs and classes, with the phantom of loan pay-offs bulging to monster proportions in their horizons.

What frontiers were their worlds they sometimes saw in headlines, newsreels, and advertisements, but the commonality of who they all were and wanted to be could only be found here, in this shabby and poorly lit cinder block structure. Maybe tonight we were all temporarily absolved in the cause of our nation, a kind of revelry in the stillness before the storm.

And the band took the stage.

Adult Civics Test I

1. Where did the word Watergate come from in the Watergate scandal?
   A   The Kennedys
   B.   Panel headed by Sen. Water
   C.   Contragate was already taken
   D.   Luxury hotel complex.

2. What recent Navy scandal caused corporate boardrooms across America to rethink their policies?
   A.   Homosexuals in the Navy
   B.   The Tailhook scandal
   C.   Outrageous overpaying for parts
   D.   All of the above
   E.   The Kennedys

3. What former Kansas Governor is famous for having a granddaughter in the Senate?
   A.   Alf Landon
   B.   Alfred E. Newman
   C.   The Kennedys
   D.   Bob Dole

4. Who will now be the leaders of the U.S. Senate and House of Representatives?
   A.   The Kennedys
   B.   Bob Dole and Newt Gingrich
   C.   Beavis & Butthead
   D.   Pat Robertson and Jimmy Swaggart

5. Is it illegal to run into a crowded fire station and yell "THEATER?"
   A. Yes
   B. No
   C. The Kennedys

6. Forcing people to pray in public schools is illegal because:
   A. Nobody knows the prayers
   B. The Kennedys
   C. It forces people to bow their heads
   D. It commingles church and state

7. How are the number of electors for each state determined?
   A. The Kennedys
   B. The price of rice in China divided by two
   C. Number of senators and representatives
   D. Decided annually by Luke and Laura

8. Which former world leader was recently diagnosed with Alzheimer's?
   A. Ronald Reagan
   B. Ronald McDonald
   C. The Kennedys
   D. Dennis Rodman

9. Can a public official hold two offices at the same time?
   A. No
   B. Only mayor and football coach
   C. Not in the same year
   D. The Kennedys

10. Pax Americana is:

A. Non-existent
   B. The Kennedys
   C. A Yankee's sports shop
   D. Latin

11. For the past 50 years U.S. foreign policy has been based on:
    A. The Kennedys
    B. Anti-Communism
    C. Aunty Em
    D. All of the above

12. Which famous eastern political family had many tragedies in the public lives?
    A. The Lodges
    B. The Adamses
    C. The Rockefellers
    D. The Bushes

    ANSWERS: 1.D 2.D 3.A 4.B 5.E 6.D 7.C 8.A 9.A 10.D 11.B 12.The Kennedys

Chapter 9

*K*ICK it. *Again*. And *again* and *again* and *again* until *these goddamn things fit.*

Which never happened. Barry had gone through all the motions. He stood at attention, learned to handle all the weapons, ran field drills, and worked towards all the opportunities allegedly waiting for him in his future - as long as he worked hard and stood proud in his rank and file. The booze was good. And if he could stay conscious after hours the books by Jack Kerouac filled in a space he dreamed of far away but were somewhat badgering, for you didn't meet many Zen Lunatics where he was. There was no outlet for the images in the theater of his mind. And it seemed all his roads fused into one huge, seemingly endless skyline of cold, wet and blue.

Be it a metaphor or just an oversight, the standard issue black shoes worn one-thousandfold did not fit - making each step around the southern Florida military base more excruciating than its predecessor.

Barry stopped and leaned against the immense flagpole in the center of the compound. With the last round of beers straining to come out and calluses abrading against the side of his shoes piss and pain took priority over duty. And for good. His decision made he stood at attention, undid the fly of his baggy white uniform, and relieved himself - all over that pole supporting 'Ol Glory as she waved over the world. Confucius would be a heck of a lot more proud should he stick to writing and playing guitar, for embellishing someone's soul with verse and music sure beat blowing them to pieces. It was less of a disrespect to establishment and country than it was a gesture to this little pit stop in his life. It was the end of the U.S. Navy for him

> *"Simply because I,*
> *I got the wrong shoes on*
> *Simply because I got the wrong shoes*
> *simply because I got the wrong shoes on."*

Baseball cap pulled down to the brow, sleeves rolled up, and crouched like a militant skater with mike cable looped in his fist, Barry kicked out his feet alternately and waved a free hand, while delivering verses in wry, appropriately high weasel-like tones. Below the stage various heads alternately rose above the mini-mob like popping kernels. Sudden lunges and occasional shoves opened temporary spaces. To his left the bassist, oblivious but always funkin' and nodding a head full of curly hair in time with the song, slid along his fretless and chipped blue ax slapping out slurs, thumps and pops. Behind them the cleaner-cut drummer churned the tempo up almost to the limit of control but kept the punk-like groove solid on a smaller, single-tomed kit. On the floor buzz-cut bespectacled athletic-type fans swung Simeon-like from the iron trusses. On stage right the shorter and more stout guitarist conveyed the melody - nodding his shaven head while cutting loose with a legion of high-pitched, appropriately squealing leads whenever possible. In all it became four fluorescent shapes capering the wily and driving songs, a sort of frantically pulsing nucleus in a circle of sound. Listening to them you knew what it meant to be down. And if you had a smidgen of soul and energy you received the transient experience of getting low. Seldom did it feel so great to feel so bad.

So there was, after all, life in this world.

Each number was answered not by clapping but with a choir of banshee howls from the little crowd. Barry never stood upright for the duration of the show; not humbled by the crowd's response but wound further up into his semi-Vaudevillian scamper and kick, one hand on the microphone, and one waving free.

They then performed their catchiest and most popular tune; a lively verse-chorus ditty that allegedly parodied a Sesame Street learning routine:

Red light green light red light go was the repeating proverb of a chorus, with most of the verse phrasing smudged but intense – and richly incoherent.

Afterwards the band was answered with not one clap but a throng of howls in unison, gratitude for the release and abandon. After the bar closed, headlights lit up the parking area outside. Several guys and gals paired off and snuck away. Which was what usually happens, for everyone else seems to have fabulous luck picking up girls when I am in the room.

I angled towards the bar where Barry sat behind a pale wake of carcinogenic smoke rising from his cigarette. His cap angled slightly up on a beading brow as he leaned in a cheerless arm pose. He gracefully granted me an interview.

Hey Barry hell of a show. I had no idea you guys had so much tight knit energy.

"Yeah, thanks. It just comes natural to us."

Do you feel a lot of pop energy in your music?

He sat bolt upright at the question before slowly sliding back down to the bar.

"Yes. Definitely. In a nutshell."

What do you see happening on the floor while you're playing?

"They dance around and get their jollies…I'm glad…I do my job every time, I get up there and do my thing, I jerk and jump and bob like they want me to, kind of like a mini hard-core pantomime theater."

Do you think you trigger the elements that make them happy when you are up there?

His brow knotted as he took a hard glowing drag off his cigarette. "No I'd say it's more a matter of people hearing what they want or need to hear. Whatever makes them look or feel cool at the moment."

So the message they are getting is not exactly the message you are conveying.

"Yeah that's it that's about right. It's like being a kind of candy vendor. Not that I don't like making people happy, it's just that they haven't developed any cavities from their favorite product yet." He was gazing over my shoulder to the now-vacant stage area. "I don't really get much freedom except when I'm writing my poetry and stories. Up there I'm a whore. It's like being a hundred miles away as I turn and prance and wrench the cheers out of them, giving them their two dollars worth at the door. I'm glad they love it. But it's far more a matter of release for them than it is learning or anything transient, and what they see and what they get is usually anything but what it is. I'm really a literary man, and I'm not sure this is my forum. It's like I test them and they fail. I don't think they would have responded like they did if they knew."

I never would have guessed. What about the Red Light Green Light song they like so much? Is that like a taste of the candy you mentioned? Could you tell me how a verse and a chorus of it goes?

"Oh yeah. Sure here, just a second. It's got a lot less to do with streetlights than the colors flashing in someone's head. Someone whose got a lot of bad urges. I mean it's not about me. At least not entirely..."

He reached for a napkin on the bar and scribbled out a phrase before politely tipping his cap, bidding me a good night and exiting alone. I began reading as the door pulled itself shut.

"Tell you what
Tell you where I want to make the cut, LSD up in your butt
Red light green light red light go
I can feel your body blown away."

A few hours later the Saturday morning sun revealed the thin gray early autumn clouds that slid in under the cover of night.

CHAPTER 10

I felt like Gideon upon the mountainside.

As I pulled onto the gravel road next to the *Mot Bleu* office I looked over the level plain of civilization feeling like the general of a lesser known cause, perched high above a militant and superior suppressor waiting for orders to attack from an unseen omnipotence eternally aloft of us all - one myself and my legion were fortunate enough to get brownie points from first. Perhaps if, like Gideon's people, we raised enough of a holy ruckus, they too would fly into a self-destructive fervor, only one that would burn into the pages of local history as a transition to something better.

True Gideon and his troops were on a bit more of an inclination than this little slope. And old Yahweh seemed to be speaking a more plain and coherent language to his zealots at the time, delivering His strategy for crushing the infidel or making them crush themselves. I've heard that God loves all his children, but He sure played favorites in that tale.

On the long and perpendicular wooden-plank porch I met one of Tom Willy's neighbors, a young athletic gent lounging on a porch swing soaking up the warm Midwestern sun and rifling through pages of what looked like some type of versed script. After exchanging greetings he offered me a seat but I politely chose to remain standing. Skipping any idle conversation he asked what my code of divinity was. I told him I was a confirmed Catholic but somewhere down the line evolved (or regressed) into a non-denominational Pantheist. His response was a simple "Okay!" before flying into tales from the doctrine that delivered him from the clutches of self-destruction. It was a story of persecuted European saints who arrived in the soon-to-be Americas just in time for the second coming of The Lord, some 400 years before Christopher Columbus landed nearby. He described the ship they used for their voyage as "a vessel of a curious nature," and I figured if Lief Erickson could have done it, so could they. He filled my arms with pamphlets and schedules of ceremony, encouraging me to venture this path towards physical and spiritual deliverance. In later days, after it became evident I was not going to show for any of these services, his salutation became a simple dirty look as I walked by.

Chapter 11

*"'Half fish,' he said. 'Fish that you were.
I am sorry that I went too far out. I ruined
us both. But we have killed many sharks, you
and I, and ruined many others. How many did you
ever kill, old fish? You do not have that spear
on your head for nothing.'"*

- The Old Man and the Sea
Ernest Hemingway

"**G**ODDAMN it."

Hey, watch out - you're spilling your drink. Alcohol abuse is a sorry curse, man.

"I'm sure you can relate. Here. You're gonna have to drive to get the next round." I hadn't planned on it, but what the hey.

Mot Bleu. An old Negro jazz musician in Wichita coined the phrase sometime during the early 1980s. For about eight years he stapled four or eight sheets together giving the run down of the local blues scene, including comments from all the local crooners and axe-men. After 20 years of playing local and regional clubs he retreated to the opaque confines of his third floor apartment, his wife four years deceased and his hands too contorted to play the Gibson semi-hollow body which rested forever in a wiry guitar stand by the side of his bed. But he did have the tapes and a stereo. Shortly after he discontinued his withered but widely read flyer, a visionary want-to-be publisher named Tom Willy breezed into town, picking up what few advertisers he had and promising to keep the tradition strong. At the moment of the hand shake the old blues man smiled broadly and leaned back in his unyielding wooden kitchen chair, believing he had really given a meaningful era in his life a lesser degree of immortality. He made Tom Willy swear he would never change the name. It meant either The Blue Note or The Blue Word, but in all our time with the mag neither of us ventured to find out which.

The creaking-spring chair was angled upwards before the browned plywood desk, where a green-screen computer monitor was royally perched. I felt the gateway to infinity buckle before my fingertips as I cracked my knuckles over the keyboard. Surely I was on a road less traveled but clearly the route to my destiny. My poor posture was getting worse, but what did it matter. Somehow I had reached a higher level of the spontaneity I thought forever lost after I finished college.

I had moved in with my new girlfriend in an apartment on the northwest side of town, a tale of tumult unto itself, but one you've likely heard or experienced a thousand times.

I entered the masthead a contributing writer about a year into publication, part of a lighthearted and certainly skeletal staff that owned fairly state-of-the art equipment - computers, page making software, and an array of vital office supplies. I was hoping to edge my way up the ranks, were there any, into a full-time editorial position. While working in or hanging around the office I got to meet nearly the whole staff, including a tipsy businessmen who contributed an anecdotal advice column to flighty questions from the public, a nomadic career water-color artist who's ambiguous vistas adorned many covers and caricatures accompanied the editorials, and a middle-aged woman photographer who loved her hobby, provided she always had a bag of good weed to go with it. On the fringes of it all was a two-person advertising sales staff to whom I was yet to be introduced.

"So what kind of rad angle are you going to give to our little rag?"

I told him I had found a little local pub that played host to a lot of lesser-known all-original acts, regionally and locally. I said I would like to focus on the local bands, in hopes of getting a slice of life into Wichita. And maybe reel in the advertising dollar in the process.

"Cool. Is it like a thrash club?"

I said no, it was sort of an after-punk club for underground bands, but they certainly provided enough material for us to write quite a portraiture of the place.

"So can you get pictures of anyone with a peace symbol on their jacket, getting their heads bashed by the police, or running naked on fire down the street?"

I don't know, maybe. But art is an expression that can't - I mean, shouldn't - be compromised or absorbed by a simpler medium for the sake of making money, so somebody like us needs to give platform to artists and performers who deserve it.

"Hey, I'll trust your judgment on that. There's probably some cool kids out there with some really good material." He patted me on the shoulder, welcoming another writer to his crew. Then his tone became low, and I could feel him over my shoulder reading the few lines I had tapped out. "Those guys sound pretty cool. But what do you know. You're just an infidel from a culture concerned only with the precious technology that paves the road to an easier, more efficient way of life with voluptuous sirens dedicated to the same damn thing." He pulled a long sip from the glass, his eyebrows descending behind the spectacles as he studied me. "You probably think Nixon was some kind of hero."

"Say, wasn't he-"

He raised a furry grey hand palm-outwards to my face, the striped dress shirt cuff emerging beneath the corduroy sleeve. From below his knotted brow the look crystallized the air in an invisible arc across the narrow space between us, halting me, and whatever thought I had just conjured. In his other hand the ice cubes jangled.

"Who was John D. Rockefeller."

I stopped typing. "Umm...Former U.S. president who was so cool he had a lot of buildings named after him."

"No. One of the wealthiest North Americans of all time, relatively. At one point he owned the majority of all oil sold in the world, triggering the passing of anti-monopoly laws, which disallowed one person to become too powerful. But of course that was back when a million dollars was a lot of money."

Which lack of is the source of most discontent and a heck of a lot of culture, I contested, spreading my scribbled notes across the table and hammering out characters across the computer screen, telling it like it is. Here came a piece I certainly would not submit to Forbes or Sports Illustrated, and that's what I liked about it most. It was time to reveal to these people just what was in the syntax of their culture, what were the fruits of their endless struggles for that damn long green. But I would not object to making my share of the rent next month.

Horoscope Off the Cusp

Happy birthday, Sagittarius! (Nov. 22 - Dec 21) Tell the iconoclasts you don't identify with your posterior. You'll never meet a can of beans you don't like if there's a John Wayne around your neck. Presence may come and presents may go. Whataya gonna do?

CAPRICORN (Dec 22 - Jan 19) Enveloping nugatory prominences can lead to an insignificant point. Tape a porcupine to your ceiling.

AQUARIUS (Jan 20 - Feb 18) Take the Eucharist with your butcher. Nip someone in the bud. Globular clustering is favored. Venture forth, never fifth.

PIECES (Feb 19 - Mar 20) Celebrate a Technicolor yawn with a friend. Play solitaire with the jokers still in, and try to grasp the double entendres.

ARIES (Mar 21 - April 19) It is important to pirouette when turning asunder. Never forget the need for lagniappes to your wait person.

TAURUS (April 20 - May 20) Prepare another's tax return for the sheer, self-abandoning fun of it. TV timeouts are the spawn of the Dark One.

GEMINI (May 21 - June 20) That's like the wolf calling the kettle in chicken's clothing a black sheep. Excuse me sir, it appears your suspenders are licensed.

CANCER (June 21 - July 22) Seeking out a mind to have something on is favored. Crenellated, Carillon, Carolingian, Colindancia and words like that have little impact now.

LEO (July 23 - Aug 22) It's the thought you count, not the count you thought, you ninny. Lissen, lissen, when kitty kat's pissin. A new acquaintance this month will be a forflushing, bamboozling, ruse of a cozen.

LIBRA (Sept 23 - Oct 22) The gigantic mastia of all giganto mastias. Being Ecumenical can keep cul-de-sacs from becoming dead ends. Forever amber nevermore, mensch.

SCORPIO (Oct 23 - Nov 31) Orotund orison is not to be heard in public pedagogy. You enjoy being stentorian and lachrymose when crapulent.

Chapter 12

"AND so in my dream this fucking zombie dog comes shuddering and shambling right at me down the same road - I'm not kidding - and there's nothing I can do to stop it - I can't move or think or anything - just sit there and stare just like my other dog did - while this demon creature comes right the fuck at me, it's flesh all rotted and falling off in clumps. And I'm like fuck this, I've seen enough, I'm definitely never going down that road again," Matt said, his baseball cap high atop his head, and the forearm of his woolly blue overcoat soaking up the little reservoir of beer spilled on the bar.

His company and audience stood in a semi-circle around his cushioned pivoting barstool, nodding and pretending to hang onto every word. Each bore the emblem of the same football team; two on their jackets, one on his cap, and one on a stained and frayed sweatshirt. Many of the local Native American tribes had joined to contest the cartoonish usage of the team name, to no avail.

The sports and car repair talk had worn thin, so these locals tuned to this new young stranger for a fresh topic or complaint. Apparently he had been drinking enough, so they were sure they could relate. Matt, who had difficulty looking up from the bar during the course of his narrative, finally raised his face and scanned the eyes of his patronage. "And I haven't been there since. That was that," he said.

The traffic broke up in southern Kansas leaving his the only vehicle on that inevitable road, headed north to his new home through that inevitable town. The emerald rectangular sign marking Harper County limits swished by. It would be different this time, he thought, memories and associations were everywhere in life, so why spend the time avoiding them. Up ahead was the old neighborhood. Soon the whole thing would be under his wheels.

With one feature byline under my belt I was fairly recognizable in the bar. That and the fact I drank there every chance I got. Local cover, metal, and dissonant noise bands floundered out their sets mostly during the weekdays, playing for a growing clientele of locals who picked up one of the 3,000 or so *Mot Bleus* we churned out the month before. Like many other great moments in life that one takes for granted when its happening, *The Rusted Bullet* had become a stingy little capsule for a great and fleeting era.

Matt fronted a band of four lads, all of recent high school graduate or dropout ages; a generation that made obscurity and angst a form of art. They wore shirts cut-off at the shoulders with hard-soled work boots fastening them to the stage. Each bore the trademark goatee of something insubordinate inside the machine. All bore this visage but Matt, whose cleanly shaven visage remained in shadow beneath the rim of the non-labeled cap he always wore just above his brow when he played his used Les Paul. His words were convoluted, but if you listened you would hear:

> *...On the way past Harper something new*
> *dead and wicked it walked into view*
> *Never again will I ever take that road*
> *Down Past Harper we're all doomed to go.*

After their last set wound down I tried to get a spot interview with the bass player, but he said, rubbing his red goatee', he was a little too tanked to give genuine replies. Matt stepped off of the stage, lifted his overcoat from the back of an old stained wooden chair and wordlessly closed it around him. When he saw me approaching in his peripheral vision he stumbled into a near sprint towards the bar, involuntarily running away for the briefest distance until cornered, when he turned smiling, lit cigarette in hand.

"Hey man I really dig your music and the CD you guys just put out."

"Thanks. We're still doing a lot of gigs to try to pay for it."

"Where did you get the name for you band?"

"It's a hand-held tool our rhythm guitar player used during one of his jobs. We really dig industrial names. They're perfect for the backgrounds we come from and the music that comes out of it."

"You guys kind of have that edgy driving sound - near something the major magazines have a little catch phrase for. Is that sound indigenous to the West, or are you trying to stay current in your style?"

"Yeah," he said, semi-laughing, "a little of both. I moved to Seattle for a little while trying to get in with the scene there, got to go to a lot of bars and see a lot of groups, but my roommates and I couldn't get along and eventually I had to move back here with... my family."

"Do you think you'll go far with this band?"

"Yeah. This is the '90s and we're trying to bring a new edge to the sound. It doesn't matter where you are. What matters is how good you are if you're going to make it. I think we're good enough. If you're good you'll be signed someday."

"So what's that one song about? I caught something about a dog and Harper and spinning?"

For a moment he went silent and a kind of grayness seemed to pass over him, the sort of tone that appears in any great interview.

"Man, that song's about me hanging out in this bar in Oklahoma trying to tell this story to a bunch of drunk guys who barely got a word of it. Part of it refers to how loaded I was at the time. The story is about when I was a kid and used to live in Harper County with my grandparents, right around the time my folks split up. I had two dogs for like two years - one of them named Friday. One day I was hanging out on the porch when Friday wandered out on to the road and got hit by a car going about 65 mph - fucking gory scene, he lived for a few moments and walked a few steps with his guts hanging out, blood all over the place, the works. My other dog just stood there and watched. He didn't seem effected by it at all. And then, I swear to God it wasn't three weeks later, he got killed on the same fucking road in the same spot by a different car. Man, that was a tough scene for a kid to see, especially with what I was going through at the time. And then, after I moved, debating whether or not I should ever again go up that road..." He sat back hard on his chair and glanced in both directions, gazing towards the little stage to finish the story. "Then..."

In his headlights two miniature flares appeared like lightning bugs in tandem, unmoving in the center of that same road. He let off the gas a little but it was not until he was right upon them that the lamps became the eyes of a dog, standing lengthwise, head turned towards the car but unmoving up to it's final moment. The passenger's side tires went up about a foot with dual grisly squashing thuds and came down as the car slanted sideways into the otherwise vacant road. Matt bounded out of his car, his cap clinging to his head in the breeze. In the dome light of his open door he saw steam exhale into the night from the freshly eviscerated furry carcass almost flattened in the center of the road, the many-colored organs and gore still sliding and oozing along the dual yellow lines. Matt turned his head, slid behind the wheel of his car and sped down the road, not looking back or considering what others who came that way might find.

After we shook hands he hopped off the barstool and picked a spot in the myriad of band flyers to push open the plywood door. The rusted spring noisily snapped the door back. With that, his first interview done, he was off into his world of optimism, armed with his God given acumen and above all, confidence.

I just have to get off of this road, he thought. And for the last time. For the very, very last time.

The men slurped the foam off of their beer mugs and shot glances at each other. Billy Bob leaned into Jacob's ear to offer a critique of the long and loquacious tale. "Hell, this one's damn near a loon, I think."

Chapter 13

*"Truly fertile music, the only kind that will move us, that
we shall truly appreciate, will be a music conductive to a dream,
which banishes all reason and analysis. One must not wish first
to understand and then to feel. Art does not tolerate reason."*

-Albert Camus

SILENCE. *No light. A void at first, with no knowledge if the amplexus or anything previous ever occurred. The singular mass then splits into two, then four, and then eight - until each resembles a chip of fruit inside a gelatin desert. Then the tiny entities begin twitching, eager to pop free and consume the mass that was once their entirety. For the first six weeks the lengthy fan-tails propel them in waves towards the pond's lilies and weeds, to which each will adhere to survive the early stages, fear and determination always present for each in the collective or in their own singularity, just like it was 360 million years before.*

It was between sets at their regular practice place - an abandon barn on a friend's property just beyond the fringes of the city, where unpaved roads and deep parallel ditches intersected to create near-perfect square miles of wheat and milo. At times the autumn night breeze bent just enough of them to look like some large invisible form was passing over.

Mary sat in a rickety fold-out chair on the edge of the carpeted practice space, where once lamp-lit auctions and square dances were held, the structure's old insulated wiring barely able to produce the wattage of their small amplifiers. The four-piece band was taking a break after completing a new song, one they had lyrics for but was yet untitled. They were a 24-ish lot, wrapping up school and managing new families. The bassist and drummer capitalized on the conventional cigarette break while their guitarist, his bicycle racing career on hold after an untimely back injury, stood with his hand in the pockets of his windbreaker, his short-cut blond visage always smiling. He glanced over to the profile of his sister, sitting and looking out to the emptiness of the barn.

She rubbed her jaw with short unpolished fingernails, tapping her foot on the wooden-planked floor in time to the song replaying in her mind. It was a story of transformation, going beyond the fear of separation to actually become something else. Suddenly a small movement, certainly not human, cut into her peripheral vision. Startled she looked almost up to see a small green amphibian that had hopped into their space to rest, throat pulsing, about four feet away from her chair. A bead of water rolled off its ever-upward-angled face onto the floor. A gift, she thought, one that certainly won't go unsung. Hence *"Frogman"* was spawned.

While predators prowled both the sunlit surface and murky depths, the fan-tailed spawn hovered agitating beneath the wide and lethargically drifting pads.

When, in the course of another year's march across the land, the only definite signs of change was the crust of snow on ground and unmistakably low temperature, there was still a lesser traveled road of pure natural vistas I could take to the west end of town. It was a fittingly single stretch of road that went to *The Rusted Bullet* without a turn. It was the far western reach of Maple Street, running four miles unpaved until greeting the greater civilized world with a green "Welcome to Wichita" sign.

During the autumn months, while most of the surrounding land turned one of two shades of brown, the effulgent colors of the season thrived there. The trees and brush were stained a deep sapphire or singed a bright orange with just enough bare spots to blanket the area in a multi-colored latticework, the fallen leaves rolling up over the dust of your tires before secretly settling to the earth again.

But this wasn't one of those times. The winter had arrived in force and stripped each limb bare, leaving such beauty latent in a glaze of ice running off each branch like countless trails of frozen tears. The icy network scraped over a full blue-hued moon in an otherwise inky sky that followed you wherever you went that night.

I pressed as hard on the gas as my driving skills would allow. I was just happy to get out, get some beer, and hear some rock and roll. This was the day I initiated a five-day countdown for at the beginning of each week. The local radio station was merciful enough to remind us what day it was in a magnificent promo, drawing the word out long, loud, low and definite - *"It's Fffrrrrrrriiiiiiiiiiiiiiiiiiiidayyyyy."* I planned on skipping the draw glass and going right for the pitcher, my head not one foot from a blaring PA horn speaker. Just knowing where I was headed was a big part of the weekend glory.

Frost crusted on the display window but you could still make out the vacuums' four handles. Ice lined the edges of the door, so it took a bit of a tug to get inside. There the room seemed a little bright by contrast. A growing crowd milled about, shedding heavy jackets and parkas one by one as their murmur escalated to a full chatter. The little stage and all the band equipment marred with fingerprints seemed poised in a singular cover of lime green.

I headed right for the bar and ordered up my first pitcher, eager to get the evening underway. My return trip through the darkened watercolors of Maple Street would likely keep me away from the cops. In a minute I had the classic foam mustache.

I sauntered over to my usual spot on the banister seriously digging the moment, alone though I was. My girlfriend simply was not into the local music scene, but agreed to a night away from each other. The room wasn't full enough to drown out all conversation, and I could hear some girls talking at a nearby table. Far was it from me to eavesdrop, but anyone discussing the ultimate nature of things usually gets my attention.

These are the names of people who cannot control themselves, these are the few who can. *This* is just being human, *this* is an aberration. *I think it's God's plan.*

I considered the validity of any definite answer. Perhaps god kept all definitions eternally elusive so life never got boring. Were their conclusions just more signs marking the territories of their egos? Was there something they overlooked? If they turned to their own empty spaces what would come hopping out?

After about six weeks the legs appear like small buds on either side of the diminishing tail. The head and eyes develop.

We basically rushed the stage when the drummer counted off the first number. The snare drum beat was sharp and very danceable, mirth on top of ire. The guitarist raised his Rickenbacher and twanged out the stirring motif. Mary stepped forward - nearly perfectly groomed but clad in frayed jeans and cut-off top. With an occasional shriek tremoring but resonant, her child-like balladeer tones carried us through that brief period of hours helping us forget that it would soon be over as quickly as it began.

We were there, a good crowd of about 30, soaking up all the energy with our vigorous but totally unsynchronized dance. It was the sound - crisp and evasive but in spirited meter - dulcet but catchy on the fringes of dissonance, like the volatility of youth itself. Only one you could visit and experience again and again at any time, as long as you had a record:

> *"...Be strong and stand,*
> *see the way it all should be.*
> *Tell yourself you can change,*
> *I know where it went wrong.*
> *Hold still hold fast,*
> *don't look fear in the eyes.*
> *See through it's mind,*
> *don't lose twice - don't lose twice."*

At last the relief of knowing one is not alone in the struggle to change, the will to become. At last some verification that beneath your conventional veil of tears there really is an undiluted and resonant energy exerting to come out - and stay. These are the waking moments of reality, ones you don't soon forget. A crossroads of empathy and ego, wisdom known and unrealized; a ground untrodden by the predators coming at us above and below.

The band had scraped up enough cash to cut a six song tape with a glossy j-card, a package I was sure to pick up after the show. Thank goodness.

At ten weeks the massive legs remain cocked to propel the body forwards and upwards in quick long leaps, for those who would survive. The twin globular eyes pop above the surface of the pond to look upon the world as the nostrils flare, drawing air over the larynx to sing. It was the rare and perfect completion of another, allegedly the only four-limbed vertebrate to go through metamorphoses.

Chapter 14

MOUSE approached as I was deciphering faded engravings on the table before me, deep in my dharmatic ambience, hoping the December chill was keeping the beer under the driver's seat of my car cold.

"Hey dude, *whassup?!*" he said, pulling out one of the gutted-cushioned chairs and sitting down with the back support in front. His trademark grin was wide and eyes a networked hue of ruby.

"Not much, man."

"Man, I'm getting fucked up, dude, how about you?"

"Working on it. Hey, what did you think of the band?"

His eyes flashed a bewildered look, his forefinger staying on the lip stud, and then said, "Oh those guys?" as if suddenly recalling the music. "They're alright."

"Did you get into it?"

"Awww....Man, I wanna hear something heavier, something to piss me off. I wanna hear them grunt real loud up there and grind real hard, y'know, *RRRWWWOOOOAAAAWWR,*" he proclaimed, his fisted arms hooked, eyes crossed and veins popping in his neck, "so I can mosh like a motherfucker."

"So you didn't like it?"

"...They're alright. But it's old, dude, a thing of the past, it's not what's going on right now, like give me the rush, y'know? Like I wanna be happy, not sad, you know, dude? Like, there's nothing happening but right now so why bitch about it, why waste your time when you should just enjoy, you know dude? I mean like, what is happening, we're sitting here hangin' at the Bullet, there's no old girlfriends or childhood trauma going on - right, dude? ...Say, can I grab a beer off your pitcher?"

Chapter 15

FIRST he noticed the size and capacity of the auditorium. Bodies wall to wall, ceiling to floor. Truly this was the largest open-forum crowd Tom Willy had ever been part of.

Then he noticed the girls he was standing next to. They were a pair, full of youth and loveliness, sometimes chatting between each other but mostly keeping their eyes fixed straight ahead as if waiting for some spectacle to descend right out of Heaven. They did not seem to have boyfriends. This was no time to be timid.

Outdoors the summer heat was glaring down hard, driving Tom Willy and his sister into the basement recreation room of their parents' home. They had just returned from Sunday mass at one of the tall steeples dotting the Cleveland suburb, where their priest addressed topics such as the base and unethical conduct of colored people on the west side of town, and the increasing number of drop-outs at the local high school. His sister, the most adamantly religious person Tom Willy ever knew, traced all causes and effects to the basics of Christianity. If only those people knew how the good word and works of God could relieve them of their cumbersome burdens of sin. Then their attention drifted towards the huge black and white television in the center of the room, where they noticed a young fellow from Mississippi who had been causing quite the upheaval nationwide, his arms swinging and legs undulating as he sang and danced across the screen. He was performing before a tremendous mob of faces, each mouth agape and screaming out a kind of ecstasy. Fascinated by the response of the crowd, Tom Willy monitored the whole spectacle while his sister stomped and protested loudly, insisting he change channels. This was obscene. When it became evident that he wasn't going to comply, she gasped, threw up her arms, and fled full-throttle up the cellar stairs.

It was a time of unadulterated tradition that suddenly, with the appearance of this new type of music, was turned onto its ear. Years later Tom Willy described the motif of the times to a friend: "Everything that was not personal suddenly became personal...We thought we were finally doing something that would change something."

The girls had been fidgeting throughout the evening. Venue after venue followed announcement after announcement as they sat, sometimes joining the clapping half-heatedly, their eyes darting back and forth across the distant stage. After one of the latter acts wrapped up their set, Tom Willy took his chance to break the ice, possibly more. First to see how adventurous they were.

"Hi, my name's Tom. Pretty cool night, huh?" Together they glanced towards him then back to the stage. "Say, I've got tickets to an upcoming gig at Leo's Casino. It's for a really big act called The Supremes, I'm sure you've heard of them. Would either of you care to accompany me?" He had invited them to a club that booked mostly all-black acts, and the response they had been getting was phenomenal. At that show several weeks later Tom Willy smelled marijuana for the first time.

They did not respond but he felt he was somehow on a roll. "They've got this comedian opening for them named Flip Wilson, I hear he's pretty good."

"I have a friend who lives on a street nearby there," the shorter, more callow of the two finally said without turning to face him. Now he was getting somewhere.

"Yeah, I know a bunch of people around there. Let's go! Maybe we have some common pals!"

"Our parents don't like us going into that area too often," said the taller gal, her eyes not leaving the stage.

It was better than being ignored. "Hey, well, you'll be with me and couple of my friends. I'm sure you'll have nothing to worry about. We'll have a great time -"

Then they were gone. The last coherent sound he heard in the building that evening was some deejay saying 'ladies and gentlemen' and the name of the band, sparking a collective cacophony he never imagined. The world became a shriek - giant, shrill and encompassing, seeming to vaporize the girls he was just picking up on. He looked about and found he was one of many guys dotting the back of the auditorium and standing alone, the same look of shock across all their faces.

All girls had rushed the stage. The curtain went up and four young lads appeared, playing in a bare-bones configuration with outrageous hair down to their earlobes and back of their necks. Tom Willy had counted on hearing the music played live, but the best he got was seeing them move. The quartet seemed to be having a time bopping back and forth across the stage, but whatever magical sounds and rhythms they produced were lost in the ubiquitous shriek without a breath.

The curtain went back down not long after the first number seemed to end. A line of uniformed police seemed to rise out of the stage before the fallen curtain, clubs drawn while their central spokesman shouted into a microphone. He said many people in front were being crushed, and the band was not going to come back out until everyone returned to their seats.

Shooting each other quick looks, the abandon fellows in the back started a mounting chant of "sit-down-Sit Down-SIT DOWN-" and Tom Willy joined in, hoping the gals would return to discuss his offer. They never did.

Finally, after the crowd somewhat receded, the deejay introduced the band again. The collective screaming, in an even higher pitch this time, intensified when the lead singer / guitarist emerged from beneath the curtain as it began to rise. Immediately he grabbed a microphone and began shouting to the crowd, scorning and berating the police for their insolence to these good kids.

These guys are cooler than I expected, thought Tom Willy. It turned out to be his favorite part of the show, and the only part he could hear.

Chapter 16

"All you umpires, back to the bleachers. Referees, hit the showers.
It's my game. I pitch, I hit, I catch, I run the bases.
At sunset I've won or lost. At sunrise, I'm out again, giving it the old try.
And no one can help me. Not even you."

- Ray Bradbury

THEY came in without knocking. I was sitting alone before the office computer on a Wednesday afternoon, overjoyed, thinking I had almost achieved the American dream. No deadline enforcers breathed down my neck making sure I punched out the latest ephemeral statistics full-throttle for breadcrumbs. And a decent readership was under my belt, one of a much more sentient demographic than your average frothing sports-statistic addict. Work and smoke breaks conjoined with a good strong drink sitting by the keyboard as I hammered out the latest feature, one I thought even cooler than the last, certain I was somehow enabling a new evolution.

Then they came in. They were your average salt and pepper team. The man, in lengthy dark dread locks, stood with arms crossed by the door while the make-up laden blonde (it seemed) lady in a woolly overcoat came towards me with briefcase in her left hand, the other outstretched for greeting.

"Hi I'm Hanna and this is Gregg," she said, "we're your advertising team." The man by the door raised a forearm for a single wave. I took her cold and somewhat skeletal hand and introduced myself. "Oh yes I've heard all about you. I'm sure we'll get along just fine. Well here's our list of steady customers," she said before I could ask how things were going, handing me a single page photocopy, "we hope to at least double that by next month's issue. We've pretty much canvassed the north and central regions of town. But for the next four weeks we plan on canvassing the whole southern region - all the smaller local taverns and shops. And from there who knows - possibly out of town but that would mean mailing at bulk rates but with the money we bring in it should be no problem."

Sounded good. All the while her cohort kept peering behind the curtain out the door window. I asked what was out there.

"Nothin' out there," he said shaking his head, his dread locks wagging, "nothin' at all."

She continued. "You people have something good going on, but I'm hoping to turn it into something bigger - something better. I'm here to work with you on this. Still, what you guys are asking for is quite a bit. The market in this town is cornered - has been for a long while. It's going to take some hard facts to get this money flowing, probably a lot of song and dance. But don't worry - we know the way to getting this thing above the ground. We're the ones you want."

Okay! I declared, content as hell. Without further ado I again shook her clammy hand and said I was looking forward to working with her. Them. She drifted back toward her partner and they waved again together while opening the door. While walking out they both gave a worrisome look to something I could not see.

Fine! Great! I thought. I hope it all works out. I went back to writing and they disappeared.

Chapter 17

AN excursion. Trying out some of the other more established clubs in town didn't seem like such a bad idear. But all the clubs catering to the more spoiled sector of folks told the same tale; frigid princesses wearing less but usually more expensive clothing delivering disgusted looks to all who dare foul her line of sight. All but that one dreamy knucklehead who tells her how greatly civilized he is (thanks to his folks' money), how women seldom say no to him, and how a night of convulsive strutting on the dance floor to the club's pre-programmed electric house music could lead to that night of bliss she was fantasizing of. *Ooo, at last a boy with some class*.

I wound up sitting next to one of these chivalric bounty hunters at the bar, trying to study his habits. I didn't have to say a word, he said it all; his shirt opened to expose the gold chain, thumbs in pockets, and blond cowlick a tad too far above his head.

"This music does it all," he said. "This music is all you need. It's got a great beat and the chicks love it. You get a chick going to this music and when it ends you're home with her. I can't understand why anyone would listen to anything else." Beaming looks between guys and gals networked throughout the club. Spring was in full fling and I guessed the natives were feeling fertile. Outside shadows pressed against the windows.

So back to the outskirts of town, in search of something a little more cerebral, or at least representative of what the minority thought of in this culture. Not far off the south highway I found a pub that looked a lot more like a near-antique furniture store unless you knew what those faded words painted years ago were near one of the dented-up-rusted-out fire exits: *Below the Surface*.

One naked bulb illuminated the helix-shaped descending stairwell. If you were tall like myself you'd probably smack your head at least once at the landing where the ceiling dropped low and the room opened wide into an area glowing phosphorescent with a myriad of disembodied and glowing cigarette butts wall to wall. You had to get within five feet of someone to see what sort of element was drawn there. It was then I felt a little more at ease. For here some of the more significant and prevalent trends of the latter decade survived.

It was a fashion show for the downtrodden and jaded. Dark smeared eyeliner, one set of clothes worn each day, hair colored and spiked in any direction, black lipstick, poor complexions. They were the order-without-order I found identity in during my adolescent years, when I realized something was amiss; we were all part of something that would ultimately conquer itself. They were unsightly but totally at ease in the swooning, collective intoxication that brought them together, just to be themselves.

Mouse was one of these people. We discussed the rise of social chagrin and its repercussions in the latter decade.

"Yeah, dude the '80s should have never happened," he said grinning wide, fingertip at rest on the metal jewel. "Never happened, dude. What came out of it? Nothing, man, nothing. Dude, that was one of the cheesiest decades I've ever seen, dude, I'm glad I wasn't in my early twenties in the 80s dude, 'cause I'd be like, this is so cheesy, dude, like something has got to change. I'd be like, I can't stand it here, dude, like, where is a time machine?"

"So what is it about the '90s that's improved?"

In all the time I knew Mouse, it was the only moment I saw the grin slip away. The fingertip remained at the stud but the grin inverted as he gazed over everyone's head. He was actually thinking. Did he think some sort of innocence was lost? Was anyone capable of having a childhood in his day? Did subtle pleasures expire with the last guileless trend? The answer finally hit him and he looked down to our little table. The toothy grin reappeared.

"More drugs, dude...Yeah, a lot more drugs!"

On the small stage the four-kid band was ready to rip. Atop the guitarist's baby face sat ten inch multi-colored Mohawk spikes while peace and leftist symbols laid in magic marker adorned his sleeveless work shirt, with the word "Kill" scattered about his faded and frayed jeans. The rest of the band had shaved their heads to a shade. The lead singer, three safety pins skewering his left eyebrow and sweat dripping off the twin studs nestled into each nostril, stepped up to the center mike and addressed the multitude of silhouetted shapes.

"How does it feel?" he shouted into the mike. "How does it feel to know you're all fucked once again? Isn't it great to know you have the inalienable right to go to any school you want and make whatever you want out of your life?" Muttering amidst the rabble. "Just as long as you're daddy's rich." Shouts. You could see that rare fire in his eyes as he slanted the base of the microphone up and shouted into it. "And fuck the fucking establishment for taking away welfare, it may very well be the last big mistake they ever make. Most of you have probably never seen what hunger can do to someone. Well, I've seen it. It makes people crazy - it makes them do things even you wouldn't believe - ONETWOTHREEFOUR

U.S. IS HISTORY, YOU'RE ALL IN MISERY
Freedom's gone, it won't be long
'till we're all trapped in our homes
We'll be one nation, under God."

The remainder of the lyrics included values being inserted anally, and the hypocrisy of The Bible. When the ire and the breakneck cadence wound down, the lead singer sauntered over to our table, nodding off lurid glances from girls who looked like they crawled right out of a cheap horror flick. He sat down hard at our table, feet together, mouth agape next to his good friend Mouse. I wanted to begin the interview while he was fresh off stage.

"Do you sense a lot of apathy for those lyrics in this crowd?"

"A lot of what?"

"Are people getting the message in the lyrics?"

"Oh I don't know. People are pretty dense in this town. I'm just in it for the chicks."

"Does it work?"

Smiles. "Yeah. Apparently so." The jaded kittens beamed at him from across the room.

"So you think conveying that kind of message, like what you sang in your first song, to this kind of crowd can bring people together to change the world they live in?"

He leaned forward fast. A journalist loves it when they strike a nerve and their subject became anxious to talk.

"Yeah, but what you and them don't see is that there is nothing we can do about it. You see, about 10 thousand years ago we were put on this planet by aliens, as part of this huge biological experiment, and now they're just hanging out watching us for their amusement, studying us to see what we've become. And when they grow tired of us, they'll just wipe us all out."

"But what about signs of species that have devolved right here on earth within the last 100 years?"

"Yeah! Of course, but that's all part of the experiment...About three hours before the show I was having sex with my girlfriend when I looked down at her and realized I was doing it with an alien. Her disguise slipped for a second and I saw her for what she really was." He leaned on his knees, bowing slightly, and shook his head. "My girlfriend is an alien."

Mouse pulled his finger away from his lipring to motion towards his friend.

"Yeah, dude! Aliens, dude! Aliens!"

Outside all the stars had vanished and a cover of smog-laden clouds moved through.

Horoscope Off the Cusp

Happy Birthday Virgos! (Aug 23 - Sept. 22) Hey buxom babes! This year is going to bring about the oldest age you've achieved yet. So perk up those pineapple salads, keep your shoes shiny and git after it!! You'll feel a whole lot more like you do now than you did last year. So flout your success in the faces of those more corpulent.

CAPRICORN (Dec 22 - Jan 19) TAR BOOSH, CAPS!! and control the red dye. Becoming bald is moribund in a facile way.

AQUARIUS (Jan 20 - Feb 18) One to one relating is especially enjoyable if there is another person involved. Critique cricket caucuses far from frigid Francophiles, but remember that embarrassing wetness could happen to you, too.

PIECES (Feb 19 - Mar 20) Elegiac means pertaining to elegies, not eulogies, man. Johnny come lately, Bonnie come too, uh huh.

ARIES (Mar 21- April 19) Mouths don't suck people, people do. Ponder this. Porcupine passion is often a prickly proposition, but a fine wine is still like a fine wine.

TAURUS (April 20 - May 20) You may be flummoxed by another's loblolly. But remember, in some cultures it is permissible to say Tuncanchu as much as two can chew.

GEMINI (May 21 - June 20) Remember that you can be

schizophrenic and so can you. It might be the kind of year that reminds you of a previous one, but it's not. Still, you're a poet and you don't even realize it.

CANCER (June 21 - July 22) Do the Chinese splits with a friend. Have you remembered to check your caulk lately.

LEO (July 23 - Aug 22) You might find yourself treating a transvestite with a new found respect this month. Take drugs seriously.

LIBRA (Sept 23 - Oct 22) Spend some QUALITY time with those you don't like. Compare anything you like to the phenomenon of a fine patina of girl sweat.

SCORPIO (Oct 23 - Nov 21) Make an effort to really get to know your neighbor's dog. Grooving on the rubble is a favorable endeavor, but forswear all but fragrant flatulence from now on.

SAGITTARIUS (Nov 22 - Dec 21) Onassis / Crevasses / Manasses / Gym Classes. Alright, Croatians are not Alsatians and they're not Haitians, either, but are they Herzegovinans?

Chapter 18

HIS *father affixed the twin dangling chains to either side of the last plastic seat. Still crouching he pushed it forward, watching it glide empty into the cloudless sky behind the house.*

The entire set was finally together. The four slanting legs were anchored firmly in the ground. Between them the four new seats pendulated gently in the light early spring breeze. When he heard the sliding glass door open he turned to see his child come running across the wooded porch followed by his wife, her hair held back under a purple kerchief and blue fuzzy bathrobe sticking to her wet skin in the breeze. She held a slim rectangular camera in one hand, and with the other halted the child from charging down the steps too fast.

The child ran through the grass to the new swing set. He selected the center seat and immediately began swinging back and forth, pumping with his legs to new heights. His mother approached the set.

She beckoned him to come down before he reached mid-airspace. There will be plenty of time to swing after I snap just a few pictures, she said. Reluctantly the child dismounted the seat and followed his mother to a spot just behind the house. There a miniature willow tree, taken out of it's nursery bag the previous week, sprouted through the firmly packed topsoil. Indentations made by the garden spade were still visible around the slender trunk. The child stood about two inches beneath the top of the tree. Okay another one, hold on, one more, his mother said, who had been documenting the scene since the willow tree was barely above her son's knees. There will be another session, and another, the child thought, in a week or more likely days.

Just one more, just one more, she pleaded, with a sadness that came out as joy. Next to the tree the child feigned smiles in the series of flashes as his eyes wandered over to the seats swaying in the wind.

Matt slumped in the driver's seat of his car, his black gig bag in the passenger's seat next to him. His cap was pulled down low to block the late afternoon sun. A couple of his friends rode in the back seat to his gig at *The Rusted Bullet*. He was staying in a house-apartment with most of his bandmates. His father, who lived in town, sent rent money during tight times. His phone conversations with his mother were now further and more in between. After the divorce was finalized she re-located to a site much farther east. That had been a number of years ago.

When they drove by the house he lifted his cap to look out the window. There the sunlight flung iridescent arrays off the windows of his old bedroom and dining room, swathing the faded paint all around the structure in a luminous orange glow. The slender tendrils of the willow tree lay in a sort of semi-cocoon over half the slanting roof of the darkened house, the uppermost blossoms swaying in the breeze above it. Later that night Matt exhaled a long cone of smoke from his cigarette through the unblinking violet light before strumming out the edgy but resonant, lethargic but full, guitar melody:

In years, that tree will grow beyond our biggest pictures
before too long you'll see just what I mean
Trees do grow beyond our biggest pictures
Don't wait too long, 'cause now it's ten feet tall.

LIFE AMONG LOSERS

"For too long we have ridiculed authority in the family, discipline in the school, and order in the state. The freedom we have sought has brought us close to chaos. We will never have a good society, much less a great one, until individual excellence is respected again. Freedom is lost unless the values underlying it are upheld. These values are duty, responsibility to authority, and the development of mental discipline. It seems to me that society has become too preoccupied with losers. We make heroes out of the oddities, celebrities out of those who break the laws and rules. It is deadly nonsense. We dwell on losers. We must have compassion for losers...But not at the expense of our winners, our doers, our true leaders. We must spend more time standing up and cheering for our winners."

Vince Lombardi
Legendary Greenbay Packers coach

As you read this passage you may think it sets a good floor plan for reestablishing something that got lost somewhere in our development as a culture and/or species. Or it is just another faded old verse, advice from our parents forgotten as we tried to become or have something more than them. Either way, it is hard to imagine everyone heard the same thing.

At this point it should not take any inspirational prose to tell you we are struggling to understand our true values. What are our values? What good will they do? What good have the old ones done? Perhaps now these questions are more important than ever, when things that seem important to our happiness turn out to be miniature time bombs ready to ruin anyone within range, including excessive pleasure, assertion of the self, and the strife for wealth and power.

If you were to talk to someone in their late 50s, you might hear of the duty and discipline Lombardi spoke of as a standard. Then somewhere down the line a bunch of irresponsible people slacked off and dropped the baton, sending deadly repercussions through the decades, affecting us economically and socially. Denying the value of competition was deadly business, for it is conflict that stimulates growth, economy, spawns solutions, even validates one's individuality.

Until about the mid 1950s the family was the foundation of American vales. Marry once, bring two families together, work together, and set a course for those who will carry on the bloodline and hand down a similar set of values and understandings. An important part was being true to one's spouse.

Somewhere self-indulgence took priority. Those who were there could tell you it blossomed like a black orchid around the Vietnam era, when denying duty and service to industry seemed to be the key to changing the world for the better. "Me" toppled "us," and appears to still reign supreme today. "My" gratification was of paramount importance. Over half the marriages began ending in divorce, a trend that continues. It then became difficult to pass on an increasingly fading, rustic set of values.

Often a divorced person will say it is a shame their children caught the worst of it, but the couple could no longer stand each other's company. "I" wasn't getting what "I" wanted. Now generations of children grow up in search of someone to look up to, a tangible roll model to help them pull together the wild extremes of their lives. With visitation rights and sprawling careers, parents began to spend only minutes with their children each day. Just ask a child in the midst of a custody battle what he or she truly values. Losers who have yet to play the game.

Sports may be a metaphor for struggling striving to achieve something better while having fun with the darker, more dangerous part of our lives. It may be a good way to stay healthy and set a course to be successful in life, as Lombardi pointed out, but look at the money vacuum that is its true essence, how much people invest in it, and then talk about heroes and oddities. I never condemned professional athletes for striking against the owners and corporations who may be considered winners above them. Recently pro baseball teams went on strike against an administration that was pulling in figures lucrative even in comparison to their multi-million individual contracts. For the rest of us, we just enter into the game of our lives with our own struggles, and learn from out losses. But there will likely always be a question mark following the parade for any winner. Is ongoing competition really the inescapable template of life? If natural selection is the process we were born unto and must adamantly abide by, then it is likely we will follow in the footsteps of the thousands of species that are regularly eliminated from the grand theater of the world to make way for something new. As author Michael Chrichton pointed out in his dinosaur thriller The *Lost Word*, for every 1,000 species ever on earth, only one remain.

It is harder to imagine a greater insanity than war. The peace campaign of the 1960s was the first motif of a legacy that seemed to echo throughout the following decades. Although Lombardi was not specific, it is not hard to guess he hinted at musicians and artists, whom in the last several decades have become like journalists, presenting the world they see through a more complex metaphor. Perhaps this is the medium with the most authenticity, pushing no one and putting none on a pedestal. Do artists paint a veritable picture of the world, or are they the ones to blame for removing us from the invaluable equation of competition? Or perhaps there is just something missing. A collective goal of the homo Sapiens seems to be life itself, living fully in the relatively short time we have, although the means to do so can be elusive for many. Perhaps our children will reveal more to us about ourselves then we know. Why else would we invest so much hope in them?

> *"For no battle is ever won, he said. They are not even fought. The field only reveals to man his own folly and despair, and victory is an illusion of philosophers and fools."*
> - *The Sound and The Fury*
> *William Faulkner*

Chapter 19

"You are all brutally mistaken about Shelley, who was without exception - the best and least selfish man I ever knew. I never knew one who was not a beast in comparison."

-Lord Byron

IT was nearly shorts-only weather and driving into the morning sun was no easy matter. In Kansas there is little to nothing to shutter the sun as it rises, sets, and all the way in between, especially on a cloudless day like this one, leaving my brow sore from squinting all the way to work. I entered the office in the midst of a weighty discussion between Tom Willy and our very pro advertising staff. Their exchanges were immediate and to the point. Without salutations I hastily slipped between them and took my place before the computer, letting go a comfy sigh as the room's air-conditioned currents brushed over me.

In the narrower section of the office Tom Willy was sitting cross-legged on his couch, clad in his ever-casual attire with a morning picker-upper still swirling in his right hand. Mrs. Hanna stood over him, briefcase in one hand and ledger in the other, while around the bend in the wider portion of the room Mr. Gregg sat on the edge of Tom Willy's bed, his eyes fixed on something out the window.

I sat down and immediately began thumping out the next full-length feature. I had begun laying out pages and writing a lot of editorial since several of his regulars dropped off the masthead, for whatever reason. Family or chemical problems, or something as common.

Our little 8.5 x 11 inch black and white 16-page rag was really getting known in town. Bands from all over the region sent us their press kits.

People we didn't know were submitting stories and prose, and even the major metro paper had picked up on the idea that something creative, original, elusive but indigenous, might actually be happening in this reach of the plains. They spent two years running far less insightful and considerably less funny rip-offs of several of our departments, including the horoscope.

I had focused on local bands, hopefully taking an angle and using a style that was provoking, a break from the industry's inverted pyramid style, the formula for mass-processed characters that ultimately revealed nothing. That was the great thing about being a journalist. The stories were endless, as long as the cognizant roamed the earth. And giving platform some of them become pretty amazing; to hear, to write, and even sometimes read. Just as long as someone was flipping the bill for the printer.

They were talking hard about where the magazine's money was going.

"At this point we can go two ways," said Mrs. Hanna, in her usual ardent tone. "We could make more money and not expand the magazine or expand the magazine and make less money."

"I'd like to expand coverage. That might land us a few more clients," Tom suggested.

"Perhaps we should land the clients first. It is not good practice to give editorial space to those who don't already advertise with you. We mean, why do someone a favor like that."

"Oh, I'm sorry, I thought this was journalism. Perhaps if we just made things a little more interesting people would come to us."

I *tek-tek-tek-tek*ed on the keyboard lightly as possible, trying not to disturb their discussion.

"That's up to you. Right now we need cash in hand to keep this publication going."

"I guess whatever we have to do to survive. We've got a good thing going here."

"We know that, but we all need to *really* care. Well, what options do you suggest, Mr. Willy?"

The cubes jangled as the glass came down. "Who is Percy Bysshe Shelley," he asked her, slanting the look up from the couch and right into her steady expression, which went unchanged as she replied.

"Who? Percy Bizzeli? Is that someone we know? I don't think we've ever met her."

"One of the great poets in history. Influenced many other all-time greats like Robert Browning, Algernon Charles Swinburne, George Bernard Shaw -"

"A poetry page? That is not such a bad idea. Maybe we could get one or so of the coffee shops to run a monthly ad announcing poetry reading nights, and maybe we could charge each contributor like five or so dollars to print their entries."

"In 1818 his wife Mary wrote *Frankenstein*."

They were still unimpressed. "We could count on at least an extra $300 each month. Perhaps we can attach an order form to the page itself."

"You know, I think there are a lot of modern day poets whom I would pay to not submit their material." He grimaced with a hearty "Aaahhhhhrrr," after downing a slug. "Well, whatever. I trust you two. Do what you have to do keep things going, and I will do whatever is within my power to help out. Cool?"

Mr. Gregg was still watching out the window when he suddenly jumped, as if startled by something he saw. I inquired what it was he saw.

"Nothing, nothing at all, man," he said shaking his head and smiling broadly. "It's really nothing at all. Nothing to worry yourself about."

Okay, I figured. There was a lot more to do.

Chapter 20

"It's not quite as easy as it used to be," said Tom Willy, grinning tenaciously at his new drink as the barkeep placed it with a coaster on the bar before him. "When we were knocking on doors in the lower-class sections of Harlem they would be like, 'Yeah, right on!' to everything we said to them, and it wasn't tough at all to get people involved in our cause." He pulled a long sip out of the glass and held it next to his face, his chin down as the smile broadened across the sinister visage. "But now that we've moved out here and are purveying to the middle class, we're getting a whole lot less 'Yeah! Right-ons!' and a lot more, 'Get the fuck off my porches!' Especially during NASCAR races." Laughter exploded between Tom Willy and one of his canvassing crew until their glasses clinked and they drank again. "Man, what the hell are we doing? Why are we wasting our time." He shook his head, the grin briefly slipping away.

It was a hot summer evening in 1984. The entire gamut in Long Island was canvassed for the year and ETHIC was reaching out to the middle classes of the Midwest, hitting more pleasant neighborhoods one door at a time. Their object this time was to raise awareness on recycling glass bottles.

"So what's the alternative to recycling, man, I ask this fat-assed lockjaw fuck, and he's like, I don't know, plastic, and I said Yeah! That's right! That's the answer, asshole! And so what happens when they fill up all the landfills with that crap? They'll have a big toxic waste non-biodegradable mausoleum to Industrial America that will outlast every human being!

Man, wait 'till archeologists from the next master race dig up one of those. They'll think we were aliens who clusterfucked in some strange solid membrane to reproduce."

He told the tale of environmental groups concerned about landfills overflowing while major beverage producers were fighting possible new recycling laws full-tilt. They were saving .02 cents per unit by using plastic, and they seemed to have a serious problem with recycling, regardless of any environmental concerns. While several states were ready to pass a new bottle law, others apparently did not want to be bothered.

"Then this fucker kicks me off of his porch without even letting me come in and make moves on his wife."

After a few more drinks they blurted out farewells to each other and Tom Willy wove his sedan to the nearest all-night convenience store for cigarettes. A dollar in pocket change would do. He leaned into the glass door to open it and plodded flat-footed to the counter. When the young besmocked clerk handed him the boxed pack Tom Willy noticed the large pile of grey fold-out flyers next to the register. He noticed the name of the beverage company. *Oh*, he thought, *maybe they're coming around after all. Telling people to do their part as well.* He picked up one and unfolded it.

> *Don't let hippie activists take away your right to a lifestyle of convenience. Recycling laws effect YOU as a taxpaying citizen. You have earned the right to drink your favorite beverages from plastic bottles and dispose of them at your convenience. Do not let less responsible activists tell YOU to feel guilty because you work for your convenience. Stand by your local beverage company's right to produce plastic bottles for YOU.*

Still scanning the words through his spectacles, Tom Willy opened the box and lit up in front of the check-out area. He later discovered the beverage company had spent millions on the campaign. *I'd better get some rest for some more fartin' in the wind tomorrow,* he thought, exhaling a billowous cloud as he stepped towards the door.

He stopped. He turned to the counter then to the door then to the counter again. He decided. *Oh hell, he's just your average 18-year-old in the fourth grade anyway.* He approached the counter.

"Pardon me, do you mind if I take these and pass them around to my friends, and like, people at clubs and stuff? I really think people need to know about this," he said, pointing a thinning finger down to the stack of flyers.

"Oh, yeah, sure," said the clerk "I mean, who are they to tell us we have to recycle. It's fu-, I mean, messed up, you know what I'm sayin'?"

"Yeah, I do, thanks," said Tom Willy, balancing the awkward pile between his hands, leaning it on his chest as the clerk hurried around the counter to hold the door for him.

Outside he slanted across the parking lot behind an adjoining row of businesses. Near a pizza parlor / juice bar he found a faded rusty dumpster, creaked open the lid, and let the flyers fall into it with a flat thud.

He looked through the dry night air to phosphorescent lights in all four horizons. He ran his fingers through his beard and thought, do we have the manpower to get all of these in the trash? Where should we start? Distant car horns sounded faintly around him as he stood by the dumpster thinking.

Chapter 21

He *could not see her.*
She saw the hands, denim-clad arms, and finally the downward-hunched profile from behind the knotted wooden banister not far from the entranceway, his eyes fixed on the swirling solution between his elbows on the bar. She sat at one of the small round tables in the darkened area that served as a dining room during daylight hours, inside the myriad dusty footprints winding between the few tables and chairs before heading out the door; a trail accumulated thick by the evening and swept clean by morning. She sat thinking of a valid reason to finish the rather strong and occasional drink she had ordered before going home.

They could not touch him here. There were no time clocks or deadlines, no kissing up to a cast of folks who certainly weren't deserving of it. Even his wife; her ever displeased, sometimes shouting face spiraled away down the stretches of road that separated them now. The ice cubes jangled as the glass went up once more and that ever-welcome fire blossomed in his gut. He could feel it already. Already the doubt and uncertainty melted away, temporarily once again. That whole exterior shroud of criticism and rewards that was allegedly him flew off and he could feel, the fully cognizant and virtuous entity that was indisputably himself, here, now, and real. Even those better things he had accomplished in years past appeared and stood out, if only acknowledged and appreciated by him in this little corner of the world. He loosened his tie like a striped coil about his neck. This was his time. And he anticipated another and another, for it could only get better with each one.

That was when she heard that far away voice, the one she listened for always but only seemed to speak up in times of anger or with pangs of sorrow. The little 5.5 x 4" notepad opened before her, and the verse appeared between the lines.

There wasn't much left. About a year and one-half had passed since

I began writing for the magazine. We tried everything to get the revenue going; even trying to make the sales ourselves, only to discover there was a true learned skill to selling things, and neither of us had it. We even tried running an ad for new advertising people, one that looked like this:

Do you want a fun job?

WELL BECOME A

CRIMINAL!

But if you can apply or want to apply professional skills, Mot Bleu is searching for an energetic

SALES REPRESENTATIVE

to help us gain new accounts
and grow as a publication!

If you would like to earn a little (and we mean a little) extra cash on the side, develop sales skills, and help Wichita's Entertainment Journal expand, call XXX-XXXX to begin a possibly bountiful journey! Yes! We know you want to!

Please be organized and personable. Cute and cuddly helps as well!!☐☐☐☐ ✗ ♌ ♒ ♌ ♒ ℯ𝓇 &⁀ ● ⌘ ○ ☒ ○ ❖ ♍ ❖ ○ ♌ ♌ ○ ♒ ♌ 🗁 🗏 🗐 🗒 🗓 🖰 🗃 🖱 🖎 ☐

But our only response came from a near-crippled ex-con who promised to kill any potential advertiser who didn't buy.

Our own little advertising tandem had taken a powder. Without so much as a "Thank-you," "Hope it works out" or even "Farewell" they grabbed a fistful of dollars of an unknown amount (hence a lesson on the value of bookkeeping) and hit the road, leaving a stalled reporter and drunken Irish poet in the cone of an inexpensive desk light typing out a diminished list of names for that month's masthead. The circles were dark beneath our eyes and unwashed clothes sticking to our skin while cigarette smoke threaded the scene in silence. The lime-green hue of the monitor lay across our faces as the copy of more local folklore and cacophonic anecdotes strolled across our eyes, backwards character by backwards character.

One by one our clients dropped off and invested their advertising dollar in finer-run publications, ones that purported the weekly word of near-dead columnists while their advertisers hawked pricey packages over the phone - *This is the one you need! We guarantee widespread exposure and a decent turnover too, oh concerned small business owner, just like we have done for years and years and years. This is the route to go! We're the ones you want.*

It was down to an elite few to put out the paper now, namely Tom Willy and I. The writing and layout was easy. There was a little proofreading but no editing, unless one can truly edit their own material. This meant we had some extra cash in our pockets while our readership seemed to be in its prime, but without someone to really show potential advertisers what we could do for them, churning out volumes of even near-ingenious (we thought) tales became futile. There had to be something we could do, some executive decision made that would save *Mot Bleu*, some method to keep the madness going.

So we hit the bar. While the band set up to play on *The Rusted Bullet's* small stage Tom Willy took leisurely but frequent sips off his standard triple brandy (straight-up) as the pitchers of beer placed before me disappeared quick. The bar matron showed up periodically to keep our goblets full and the glass ashtray between us wanting. Many of the regulars made up a decent size crowd (without Mouse, this wasn't his bag) along with several relatively unknown college types, formerly my kind of people, seated in groups at the little booths with margaritas and sex-on-the-beaches between their fuzzy-sweater elbows. It was a true aesthetic. Kind of a chronic celebration of the in-betweens - released from the auspices of their parents and high schools while nurturing their minds with metaphor and melody, but by their own right miles away from the stoic and stringent filters of the manageable world soon to be theirs. I felt pangs of separation like thin icicles in my gut as I watched them drink and lean in to anxiously talk with one another, their wide smiles and lighted eyes a setting of near perfection. For I was one step ahead of them, my bargain sneakers wet and back of my ears less dampened during these first few years in the real world. Fortunately Tom Willy hadn't completely gone the distance yet, either.

He offered a social commentary on the gathering of modern youth adjacent to our table.

"Man, I want to lick her all over that tight little body. But Jesus Christ, she could be my goddamn granddaughter," he said, motioning towards the young brunette chattering intently to her friends.

"What do you think they are talking about? Sports? The new cars their daddies bought them? Their jock boyfriends? What is the fate of the free world that will soon be theirs?"

"I don't know. Maybe they're cool, you never know."

"Man, I hope they're not cool like us. 'Cause if we don't sell some ads quick we're gonna be some cool-ass homeless starving fucks." He laughed and pulled another long slug off his drink.

It was hard getting into the spirit of things. All the elements were there for another evening of exultation and abandon, but I had developed this awareness of short periods of time, like somehow their value was creeping upwards while various beginnings and endings narrowed. I was worrying about the near future, specifically the coming month. The potential aridity our cause seemed to resonate around me, and the beer offered little solace. But for tonight, what the hell.

"Hey. Don't look so glum. No one said it was going to be easy. What do you think one of your Faulkners or Kerouacs or underground guitar heroes would say if you walked up to them and said, 'Hey man, you're my role model. I wish I had your life.'"

"You wouldn't want to be me?" I answered like a question.

"Yeah, man! Probably. You never get the whole story on them legendary folks. They never tell you what they undertook to do the things they did, or what it would take for you to do it your own way." With his right hand he pulled his drink off the table and waved it about like a torch, beads of booze sliding down either side of the glass. "Here's to you! I hope you make it someday, man, I really do. But at best you're going to be a barely-sung paradigm in a literary wasteland. Who are the great authors and artists of today? Who are the acts to follow? Horror, crime and romance authors? What are they talking about? What do they mean? Does anyone know? Does anyone give a flying fuck?" A fuzzy chord rang out while the guitar player tuned. "Man, I used to be able to start a cool conversation with anyone by just mentioning somebody like Kurt Vonnegut, or...or - even Henry Kissinger. Now I'm afraid to go up to someone and say Thomas Jefferson." He fired the look across the floor to the table of students but went unnoticed. "Yeah, we talked like kids too, but at least we were concerned. What do they stand for? They probably were told and believe and will pass down to their kids that Nixon was some kind of hero. And thus the prick goes to his grave with a reputation unblemished after all, goddamn it!" he exclaimed slamming his south paw on the table, sending the amber panes of beer in my pitcher and draw glass into synchronized pendulation.

"But wasn't Nixon the one to open relations with China, hold off the cold war with Russia, and end the war along with all the civil conflict right here in the US?" I said. "Aren't those some pretty major accomplishments?"

"Yeah," he acknowledged unwaveringly, "but it was hip to hate him at the time. You know, like pictures of him walking on the beach with his suit on and stuff like that."

I considered, and asked again.

"And what of the vets returning home? Why did you throw rotten food at them? Don't you think they made the supreme sacrifice, so you and I didn't get drafted, and should be honored for it?"

"Yeah, but that was pretty popular to do at the time, too. Oh what difference does any of it make now. In about five years eight companies are going to own everything, anyway and we'll really get told what to like and what not to." The look angled down as he returned his drink to the table. "Well, you probably will anyway."

"I don't know, things always gotta get bad," I paused for a voluminous burp that for a moment killed all conversation in the bar as my eternal optimism reared its ugly head once more, "before they get good again, you know."

This seemed to energize the look. "Hey, have you noticed you find more and more of the modern pop music, like that alternative crap, in radio ads, TV commercials and movies now?"

"Yeah."

"Industry thwarts the art again. And what about that indie-type music you like so much? I don't hear a lot of that on the radio anymore. It seems that Christian bands are playing that kind of music now, of all things. What do you think of that? Does that suck? Is that a bad thing?"

".... I'm not sure."

Tom Willy administered that accusingly-certain glare as hard as he could, steadfast but teetering as he fought to remain on the chair. Behind the twin rippled wakes of cigarette smoke in the barely ventilated bar he took on the scowling but haggard visage of Skunk Johnson, the solo western pioneer on a crusade to be free of all the misgivings of others. Only at the end of this story he was unable to outwit his adversaries, and had little territory to call his own.

On the small stage the band lumbered back, eyes closed, beginning the resonant mid-tempo motif. Then they lurched forward, curled into their guitars and drum kit as if diminished by the music, as Mary arced upwards with the microphone to sing, her eyes still closed. Her features and hair were violet in the lower monotone footlights:

> *"Now I find shelter in the taste of the painkiller-*
> *So now there's something we share, but he is unaware.*
> *I'll drink tonight, but through his pain,*
> *avoid all that's real, all that's sane.*
> *No, I can't let it go-*
> *I can't let it go."*

Chapter 22

EVERY time the east door opened the world had it's fleeting opportunity to see what bands were playing or had played there, on the myriad of fliers posted over one another, before the rickety steel spring sluggishly pulled it closed with a thud.

Only upon the inside side this warm summer evening, as it creaked open at least 100 times, was something momentous. On the 12"x 24" flyer, above the black and white picture of the band creeping through the wreckage of a dilapidated and formerly prosperous chemical plant, arced these words, huge and amateur:

Last Night For the weasels?

Apparently the band had decided to call it quits when the nefarious "creative differences" imp stole onto the scene. But once word got out that soon no one would be able to take their groove for granted the place filled up - packed wall to stage with all the regulars and a whole cast of others I did not recognize. With a one-person waiting staff getting the ceremonial pitchers of beer was no simple task - So to play it safe I ordered two at a time. Perhaps this was a scene Kerouac would have loved, if only the joy and celebration had not become an escape, and the things many of them clung to in their lives were tokens of freedom, and not desperation. Later a gal pointed out to me what a sexist slob she thought Kerouac was. I did not understand.

The band didn't waste time ascending the little stage for the last time. The bass funk-groove was low, the guitar a squealing rodent and the beat driving and releasing. Barry, his cap down one last time, scampered, squatted and shouted through the colored darkness. The synchronized lights pulsed around the perimeter, creating the illusion of endless chase, casting their Christmas colors on an area packed wall to wall with colliding young bodies, streams and puddles of beer, clinking and smashing draw glasses. Those of us who were regulars fought our way screaming and howling to the front. There we sang out the words of every song (those we understood) while members of the various bands took turns swinging like anthropoids from the steel trusses, terminating their turn by plunging head-first into the crowd, who sometimes broke their fall. Complimentary bruises and abrasions were handed, elbowed and kneed out everywhere. The last I saw of Mouse was two flailing arms knocked asunder as they reached inwards for the ring on his lip, descending into the mob with a diminishing cry of, "Dude! Dude....dude...." Above the band the gelled lights shifting back and forth in their regular patterns. In this capsule of funk and rancor I wondered how far the sound carried beyond the cinder blocked walls; if it ever did, if it ever would.

Crowded up to the little stage we all raised one sneaker or sandal (rights and lefts alike) and together sang out our individual "wrong shoe" experiences in unison during that song. Or together savored the joy of being a misfit, just for that one night, and likely for the last time in our lives. Then in that trademark poise Barry scurried back and forth not two feet above our heads letting us know just where he stood. And it seemed we could all relate.

"Everybody wants to know why I don't comb my hair,
I don't care I don't care.
Everybody wants to know what we're still doing here,
Free beer free beer.
Everybody wants to know why we just don't go home,
I don't know, I don't know.
It's not easy - being me."

And when all was sang and done, all the metaphor rhythm and frenzy expired, the drummer rose from his throne and presented an anecdotal lunar gluteus max to the crowd. That we could have lived without.

Later, around last call, I asked Barry where the wellspring of their prodigy lay. It was tough to say if everyone who attended their shows felt the same as Barry, but there was little question for him what the enduring element was.

"The music came strictly from the dick," he said. "It was about pure sexual energy. We were about drinking, dancing, and having a good time."

"Then why did this group like it so much?"

"They heard what they wanted to hear. What we heard in the media that worked we regurgitated to the people. Like I told you, what they heard isn't exactly what they were getting."

"Does that explain the cap and all the crouching?"

"The reason I did that is so no one would see me, how nervous I was. It seemed like a routine but it was all real, I tell you. Like Elvis I got shaky legs."

Is that what the crowd heard? If it was a libidinous thing for some or if it wasn't, never again did such a phenomenon appear in that town, likely to this date. From then on it seemed local clubs were filled with cover or country venues, with the occasional modern metal band who pumped down low the tide of misdirected anger and pangs of compulsion. Maybe it was a kind of a transformation from unsupervised fun to the flagrant ugliness of youth. Or maybe I was just getting old.

I did not want to leave. Not because of the beer or partying, but because I knew in our passing the unseen winds would arrive to pull the flyers from the walls, sweep the PA from the stage, the under-age kids from their common ground and do all within its naturally selective powers to dislodge every iota of small-time significance that almost took root there. Was it Jung or Freud who didn't believe in coincidence? Regardless, it came as no surprise the end of *The Bullet's* alternative scene coincided with the last issues ever of *Mot Bleu*. There was little question what the motif of this story would be -

> *"Last night, I don't remember a thing*
> *Last night last night."*

Adult Civics Test II

1. The Dairy industry and all its outlets are owned and regulated by the Federal Government.
    A. True
    B. False
    C. Only Federal farmers

2. The governor of Kansas right now is:
    A. Chelsey Clinton
    B. John Brown
    C. Margaret Thatcher
    D. ...It's not Finney, is it?

3. Dan Glickman is:
    A. Employed by the Federal Government
    B. The amalgam of all U.S. politicians
    C. A creation of Gary Trudeau
    D. Presently assuming the alias of Sarajul

4. The breakthrough television show of the 1960s was:
    A. Star Trek
    B. Leave it to Beavis
    C. Roy Orbison's Stock Car Races
    D. The Animaniacs

5. Wichita, KS is known for having a big:
    A. Sewer system
    B. Indian icon
    C. Drug problem
    D. Catheter

6. Pork rinds were to George Bush as Arabia was to Powell's Colon:
   A. All of the above
   B. ...It's not Finney, is it?
   C. Senior

7. Newt Gingrich drinks:
   A. False
   B. With his mother
   C. Wine
   D. Through a tube in his trachea

8. The leader of a town hall meeting is:
   A. The mayor
   B. The major
   C. ...it's not Finney, is it?
   D. Whoever gets there first

9. The "good guys" in the Bosnia-Serbia-Montenegro-Croatia-Herzegovina fighting are:
   A. The U.N. forces
   B. The Supreme Being
   C. The defense at the O.J. Simpson trial
   D. The IRA

10. The U.S. Supreme Court has ruled that term limits:
    A. Shall not be imposed by the states
    B. Shall not be stated by the imposed
    C. ...will not be Finney, will they?
    D. What was the question?

11. The seat of our national government:
    A. Smells like Clinton's butt

B. Is shiny
C. Is Washington, DC
D. Let's attack Al Gore

12. The correct title of someone who speaks at length to prevent or delay passage of a bill is a:
    A. Lounge lizard
    B. ...it's not Finney, is it?
    C. Filibuster
    D. Hey, dude

13. (Food question no. 1) The term "Cornish game hen" comes from:
    A. Roger Cornish
    B. A foul up in European sports
    C. England
    D. Garbage in, garbage out
    E. You suck

14. The only female governor in Kansas, for as long as anyone cares to remember, was:
    A. Elma Broadfoot
    B. Ru Paul
    C. Nancy Kassebaum
    D. Vanilla Ice

ANSWERS: 1.D 2.D 3.A 4.D 5.B 6.A 7.E 8.A 9.C 10.D 11.C 12.D 13.E 14. ...It's not Finney, is it?

CHAPTER 23

*"I believe, my shirt is wearin' thin
and change, is what I believe in."*

I Believe
R.E.M

THE striped awnings flapped noisily above the sidewalks and below the rusted-brick apartment windows of Douglas Street in mid-town. Their bluish hues blocked the sun but faded a little each year, as the names of the clubs beneath them, as well as their owners, came and went.

We opted to hold our final editorial meeting at one of these clubs in this better tidied environment, finding it hard to face what *The Rusted Bullet* had become after swapping ownerships.

It was over for *Mot Bleu*. We had just put out one of our best issues ever, printed on cheaper, less glossy paper, though packed from banner to back page with reviews, poetry, announcements, and full-length features on musicians and artists - a fitting sort of epitaph. We received many letters from reverent readers but no one was stepping forward with big wads of cash to help out. Without the long green coming in our once extensive masthead was reduced to a scant list of contributors. We did not have to send them any special notice of the mag's demise.

Now in the onset of the late autumn chill I was on the job hunt again. Tom Willy was headed out even farther west, to a small town near Denver, where his sister would rent him a room in the basement of her elegant suburban home.

But we would not allow the future to arrive, at least for that night.

There is no better time to savor a moment then when you know it will soon be gone, which was likely the central philosophy of all jubilant alcoholics.

So why make exceptions now. Amidst the better off, more adult after-work crowd we sat at a round table, our legs beneath a spotless tablecloth with a slightly more expensive variety of beer and brandy before us. We had been comparing the social tribulation in America during the last six years to that of the 1960s, namely race riots, student protests and battles fought for whatever causes. Those incidents I was not around for or aware of I quietly complied with, nodding my head as Tom Willy told the stories. It did not take long to conclude that neither of us were sure if this modern era was finer or worse; if things had changed, or if anyone knew what they could be protesting.

After a seven dollar pitcher or two I got onto one of my more prevalent whines; the digestion of all aspects of life into the formulas of industry; be it art, religion or any perceivable force or unspoken thing, just to make a dollar. I suggested we capitalize.

"Man, so now what? How about we start a metal magazine. Oh wait, the metalheads don't have any money. How about a gossip rag? Or better yet - an alternative sports tabloid, like there is some alternative to athletic competition. How about Hunting Wildlife Unto Extinction, Meet Your Dream Sleazeball or Christian Capitalist Quarterly?"

"I know. How about, 'Someone Give Me a Fucking Job?" Tom Willy laughed, administering the look through every slurred syllable. "I'm sorry, man. I'm just kidding."

"No, its all right. Its time to get back to the making a living thing anyway, just like I did in Chapeau. And just like everyone else that seems to be stranded here."

"Stranded? Where? In the city or on the Earth? Like any glimmer of hope to get people interested in the world around them remains. Like someday we can tear their eyes off NASCAR and get them involved in something worthwhile." The look endured, but suggested sarcasm. "Man, you can be pretty condescending,"

"Yeah. I mean - I think Freud's pleasure principle is totally perpetuated in this culture, just to keep cranking out the ravenous consumer – clinging inseparably to the ego, which I always thought was the bane of the world. It would be great to make acting in the interest of a larger group the norm, without being called a commie, anyway." The look. "Man, I hope I'm not condescending. I really do."

"What larger group did you have in mind? Yourself?" He glanced over at a cluster of t-shirted, baseball-capped males seated at the bar who just might fit the description of those I might be inadvertently condescending to. Who may in turn be not at all impressed by myself; if only I had a case to blame them.

"Those guys are probably the prototypes of what they want us all to be like," I said.

"Oh yeah? A prototype, huh? What kind of prototype is that?"

"Just the type whose appraisal of self-worth is measured by the things he can afford. How hard he hangs on to every sports datum, how macho he is to his silicon-implanted wife. A kind of king of his domain on a tiny pulpit constructed just for him."

"Okay. Dramatic. And who exactly are 'they?'"

Fortunately I had been prepared for this one, though it had taken some heavy thinking to come up with an answer.

"I don't think it's The Government as much as it is the corporations who cram all these false values down our throats so we feel we can't control ourselves, and that we have to buy, buy, buy all the worthless shit we can cram into our physical spaces, and pay ridiculous prices for it." A young college-type gal stepped through the door, immediately bopping with her smiling blonde effervescence to the electronic tones that erupted over the little PA. Our eyes followed her as she passed our table.

"Hey people don't buy what they don't want," he said, watching the girl swagger to the bar. "I'd like to cram into her physical space. I would suffer a little radiation for that." I wondered if that gal had ever read Kerouac.

"But is it really that way? Are you certain there's really a 'they?' Maybe everyone made it this way, by getting off on the simple things they've got. Maybe they believe in it. I mean perish the thought that times may actually be better, and there's room to enjoy the subtle things in life, regardless of who's got what inflated ego. Maybe this is the way it should be, and there is no one to blame for our problems but us." We looked to the bar as the girl approached the group of lads and engaged in long, blushing and fatuous smiles with them. They likely wouldn't start discussing Kierkegaard or Nietzsche. She would likely go home with one of them, perhaps for good. "I'm sure you've heard the expression -"

"Ignorance is bliss?" said I, with an unheeded look of my own, harboring a surge of the closest thing to jealousy I'd ever admit to.

"Yeah. Right. That may be true, but I think if you make your life into what you conceptualize it to be, then that in itself is bliss, too. Maybe you need to get into a little more competition - spice up your life, validate your own existence." I frowned. "We used to have this saying, 'We have been thwarted by a deviant culture, and it is us.'" He looked to me for a response, but I was still occupied sulking. "Oh, don't be so cynical. Laugh, man. You can't let life swing by you like that."

I nodded sullenly. After a hearty pull off of his drink Tom Willy fixed a menacing look upon me, but no longer amused I looked away.

"Who's Brian Dowling?"

I don't know that Hindu bald dude who used peaceful resistance to liberate India from the Canadians.

"No - backup quarterback for the Boston Patriots during the early 1970s. Became "BD" in the comic strip "Doonesbury." I was still not impressed. "No, man," he laughed, "don't beat yourself up for it. You just have to tell people the same thing. Don't be embarrassed to read. Don't be embarrassed to think. Don't be embarrassed to say. It's not embarrassing to express what you think and feel. What's embarrassing is getting all psyched up out of your mind for the new hockey team in town. That's embarrassing." Outside in the street a driver punched hard on his car horn at something. "Just never be sure that you know everything. If you think you know something, anything, you need to check it out, because you just might find you didn't really know what you thought you knew. Man, I'll tell you, you are so naive. But I have a lot of respect for you. I'm just so sad for you because your life has not been as rich as mine." I decided to never contemplate the validity of that statement.

But it seemed to cheer up Tom Willy. Again comforted by his own off-center certainty, or simply satisfied with his closing sentiment, he laughed loud, rose from the table, adjusted the lapels on his corduroy jacket, and hobbled out beneath the starry night sky. He pointed his key at the lock of his car door, and squinted as if trying to aim. He looked up at me as I stood in the half-opened door.

"You're an all right guy, I mean it. But you just barely escaped being an idiot." A wide, more universally maniac smile. "Oh wait a minute - am I being condescending?"

I heard his laughter over the engine as he roared west down Douglas Street. Just before he disappeared into the thicket of buildings and streetlights I could make out a silhouette of an arm slide out above the roof with one digit raised, and could faintly make out the echo of that all-understood two-worded phrase as the arm attached to it pendulated, for all glancing out their darkened or lighted window panes to see. I glanced down at the soft pack of cigarettes I purchased earlier trying to assess my need, or were it desire for one, and headed east under the awnings towards my shabby white car.

Chapter 24

"Hey watch where you're spittin' that stuff."

"I got a dollar. Match you for one and we'll git eight songs."

"Sounds like a bargain. Make sure it's all country though, or you ain't got a deal!"

"Keep yer britches on. We ain't got no other options anyhow, thank the Lord. Here. I'll pick four and you pick, um, four."

"Cool. We all pretty much like the same ones anyway. I can't wait to get out there and dance! Country's the only way to be, only route I'm ever gonna go."

"I'll attest to that. It's got twang, it's fun to get drunk to, it's about real life, and you can do the electric slide to it."

"Hell yeah!"

"Right on. I can't understand why anyone would listen to anything else."

Chapter 25

NEVER held or known beyond its own confines / A brilliantly woven tapestry, one never to unfurl. That was it. So that was that. I can hear the formaldehyde circumventing the perimeter of the vacant skull - along the walls, behind the bar counter, and through the taps to finally puddle into our dusty draw glasses. The pub had changed ownerships, and apparently after everyone under 21 was shunned from the place, the owners no longer made enough money to support original local bands. I heard they had moved on to bigger and better things.

The bands I covered were now all defunct, anyway. As time became more valuable they shifted focus to school, family and jobs. Or they just vanished. I heard the metal bands were planning to descend on the site for a festival titled *"Kill The Bullet,"* but apparently none of the pub's former clientele would be around to appreciate it. I heard Mouse had let his lip piercing grow over and was now managing a restaurant somewhere. Matt had gone onto higher education. The weasels band had rejoined, changed their name, and were playing... somewhere. I even called the Chapeau paper to find the California Archetype had thrown in the mass-produced towel and found gainful solace somewhere with his church. Apparently he was satisfied with trophies the state press association awarded him for praising God, thriving business, and war against non-Christians.

For me it was time again to fill a niche carved firmly into the catacombs of this world. Surely somewhere there was a levy of new sports info waiting to surge, and I need convince some stranger I'm the man for the job. My girlfriend was thrilled with the notion.

As the final thud of the country band fell I take one last look around, soaking up an eye load of what is left; the little stage area, bowed pool tables, less legible engravings, and the Christmas lights running around the perimeter. The glass of formaldehyde between my elbows has gone flat, and I opt not to finish it.

    I make my way across the fractured asphalt to my car, another abstract image flickering over the steadfast line of vacuum cleaners. Along the rows of orange streetlights curving throughout the city I can hear the air, rushing secretly from place to place. The traffic is silent this evening.